DIRECT HIT

An explosion in front of the Audi brought it to a halt and spattered it with dirt. The car half vanished in the gathering smoke.

As Frank watched helplessly from the roadside, a third missile screamed down. Shock waves hurled him back as the car went up in a ball of fire.

"Joe!" Frank called as he picked himself up off the ground. "Joe!"

No sound came from the Audi except a steady crackling, and no movement but the dancing of the flames.

Books in THE HARDY BOYS CASEFILES™ Series

Available from ARCHWAY Paperbacks

THE HARDY BOYS CASEFILES NO. 14

TOO MANY TRAITORS

FRANKLIN W. DIXON

AN ARCHWAY PAPERBACK
Published by POCKET BOOKS
New York   London   Toronto   Sydney   Tokyo

AN ARCHWAY PAPERBACK *Original*

An Archway Paperback published by
POCKET BOOKS, a division of Simon & Schuster, Inc.
1230 Avenue of the Americas, New York, N.Y. 10020

ISBN: 0-671-64460-2

First Archway Paperback printing April 1988

10 9 8 7 6 5 4 3 2 1

TOO MANY TRAITORS

Chapter

1

"COME ON, FRANK, show a little life," Joe Hardy said. "We're landing soon."

He glanced out the plane window, his blue eyes eager for a glimpse of the Spanish coastline. Joe loved the rush of takeoffs and landings. And, as he stretched, he was glad that the long flight from New York was almost over.

"Hey, *Frank!*" Joe repeated. A year older than Joe, Frank Hardy bore little resemblance to his brother: Frank was slim and an inch taller than Joe. Frank's hair was brown, Joe's was blond.

Finally Joe shook Frank's arm, and Frank opened his eyes. He'd been listening to music on his new Walkman. Now he slipped the headphones off his ears and let them dangle around his neck. "Take it easy, Joe," he said. "That's

1

what we're on vacation for, remember? To relax.''

"You're right," Joe admitted. He was tense because he was expecting trouble. Lately trouble had been coming to them out of seemingly innocent situations. A visit to the mall had thrown Frank and him into an assassination plot. A plane ride had become a hijacking. Even a simple party had turned into a bizarre murder attempt in their last case, *The Borgia Dagger*.

Even though they were only seventeen and eighteen Joe and Frank Hardy had fought more crime than most big-city policemen. They just seemed to fall into it—either in their hometown of Bayport or anywhere that they traveled.

"I'd have more fun if you'd talk to me, Frank. You've barely said two words since you won that Walkman. All the way across the Atlantic, you've just sat there, plugged into—"

"I like listening to music." Frank held an earphone to one ear so he could listen to Joe with the other. "Besides, this is a prize—just like this trip. And I intend to enjoy *all* my winnings."

Joe slouched in his seat and looked over at his brother and smiled about Frank's recent good fortune. Frank had entered a contest while he was ordering some computer supplies by mail. Several weeks later he learned he was the winner of an all-expense-paid trip for two to the sunny Spanish paradise called the Costa del Sol.

The first prize included the trip, complete with guided tour. But among the other goodies were the Walkman and a supply of tapes to play in it.

Joe spoke again. "I think you brought me along only because Callie wasn't free."

"Come on, you know that's not true," Frank said, shrugging off Joe's teasing. He knew Joe finally had a grudging respect for his girlfriend, Callie Shaw. Because even Joe had to admit that it was Callie who'd saved them all during the Borgia Dagger case.

Frank teased his brother back. "I'd have offered the trip to Mom and Dad if they hadn't gone to Chicago. Lucky for you they took Aunt Gertrude with them."

"She doesn't like the beach. All that sand is bad for her shoes." He grinned. "Boy, I hope the Spanish beaches live up to their reputation." He closed his eyes and imagined the girls.

The wheels touched down on the tarmac of the airport runway. Within minutes the plane had taxied to the gate. Soon Frank and Joe were heading down the aisle toward the door.

"So long, Joe," said a smiling red-haired flight attendant as they stepped through the exit. "Hope I see you on the flight home."

"Me, too, Cindy," Joe replied. Waving at her, he followed his brother along the exit ramp.

"When did you two get so friendly?" asked Frank in surprise.

Joe tugged lightly on the headphones dangling around Frank's neck. "There's a lot you miss when you have these things plastered to your ears." He winked at his brother and set off for the customs line.

After clearing customs, they walked into the terminal.

Joe glanced around. "I thought somebody was supposed to meet us."

Frank grabbed Joe's arm and pointed. "There's our man."

Ahead of them stood a sandy-haired man of about thirty, his arms and face well tanned. The man wore black slacks and a red- and white-striped shirt, and he held a handwritten sign. The scrawled letters read "Hardy."

"Here we are," Frank called. The man spotted him and lowered his sign as the brothers approached. "I'm Frank Hardy," Frank said. "This is my brother, Joe."

"Welcome to Spain," the man said, smiling. "I'm Martin Chase—call me Martin. I'm your guide. For a minute there I wasn't sure I'd find you."

"But I thought this kind of thing was everyday stuff for you guys," Frank said.

Martin shrugged, embarrassed. "Not for me. I'm a writer, and Málaga is a nice place to write. I guide English-speaking tourists to keep the roof over my head and feed myself."

4

"What do you write?" Joe asked.

"Journalistic stuff," Martin said. "Which reminds me—you are Fenton Hardy's sons, aren't you?"

"How'd you know that?" Frank eyed him.

Martin smiled sheepishly. "You'll have to forgive me. I do a lot of crime writing, and I'm something of an armchair detective. Your father is one of my heroes, a really exceptional investigator. I've read about all of his cases." Martin studied their faces. "You know, you both look a little like him."

"Well, what do you know?" Frank said. "Dad's reputation grows all the time."

Martin nodded. "Is that all your luggage?"

"This is it." Joe picked up one of their two overnight bags. "We like traveling light."

"Let's go, then," Martin said. He led the way through a crowd of perplexed tourists, blasé world travelers, and relaxed residents. Outside, Martin stopped beside a long black limousine.

The driver hopped out to open the back door. He wore a dark suit and chauffeur's cap. A thick black beard masked his face, and sunglasses hid his eyes. While the Hardys got into the backseat and Martin climbed in front, the chauffeur loaded the bags into the trunk. Then he climbed behind the wheel again. All this he did without uttering a word.

"To the hotel," Martin ordered. Soon the big

car was weaving through the fast-moving traffic, heading toward downtown Málaga.

The city amazed Frank. He had expected the old stone buildings, but the park-lined boulevards and the plazas with outdoor cafés and fountains were a surprise to him. It wasn't the quaint little village he had expected, but a beautiful city that mixed the Old World with the new.

The local bullring, the impressive Plaza de Toros, came into view. Then it gave way to baroque-style churches whose ornate towers gleamed hot white in the bright sun.

"Know much about Málaga?" Martin asked, turning in his seat to look at the Hardys.

"Just what we read in the brochure," Frank began.

"This place is an old port founded by the Phoenicians some three thousand years ago," their guide said. "There's a lot of history in this old town."

Joe said, "I was hoping they'd have discos here too."

Martin laughed. "Don't worry," he assured him. "I suggest you work off your jet lag with a good night's sleep. Then tomorrow we'll start on the *real* tour—including a couple of the better discos."

The big black car rolled to a quiet stop in front of an impressive old stone building with a red-tiled roof. They slid out of the car and Martin escorted them into the large, cool lobby of their hotel. They passed sturdy wood and leather chairs, tall urns filled with bright flowering plants, and huge oil paintings of Spanish nobles of centuries past. At the oak front desk, the hotel clerk welcomed the Hardys and handed them registration forms.

Frank set his tape player on the counter. Before he started filling out the form, he noticed Martin admiring it. "Want to try it?" Frank asked. "I won it as part of the contest. It's the latest model."

Nodding, Martin slipped on the earphones and switched on the machine. "Thanks." He grinned as the music began to play, and as Frank and Joe registered, Martin paced the lobby, listening.

"This is great," Martin said as the Hardys approached him moments later, room keys in hand. He started to hand the player back, then pulled it away just before Frank could touch it. "I don't suppose you'd part with it?"

"Not a chance," Frank said. He put out his hand and Martin reluctantly handed it back. Frank clipped it to his belt.

"Our rooms are on the third floor," Joe said.

"So is mine," their guide replied. "This way." He led them to an elevator and pressed the button next to the wrought-iron gates. "Your tour will work like this—tomorrow we'll check out the city of Málaga itself."

7

He nodded excitedly. "You've got to visit the cathedral, Gibralfaro Castle, Picasso's birthplace, the Fine Arts Museum, and, of course, a bullfight and a flamenco club. And, you can't miss eating paella at Pedro's."

"That sounds like a week's tour, Martin," said Joe.

"There'll be days to take it easy," Martin assured him. "There's the beach, and some little towns—Torremolinos, Fuengirola, and Marbella—and a stop for fish at La Carihuela, an old fishing village that—"

The elevator arrived and Martin paused, tugged the door open, and held it as the Hardys carried their luggage in.

As the door slid shut, Joe heard footsteps running for the door. Without thinking, he pushed it back open.

Two pretty blond girls got in and smiled at Joe. Then they started whispering together, sneaking peeks at him. Joe couldn't make out what they were saying, except for an odd word here or there. German? Swiss? Swedish? He couldn't decide.

He smiled back at the girls, about to say something to them, but then Martin started in again.

"For the rest of the week," the guide said, "there'll be day trips to Granada, Seville, and Ronda, and you don't want to miss the hydrofoil over to Tangier. Then there's—"

8

"Hey, I thought this trip was for relaxing," Frank said, smiling. "You're going to run us ragged."

"Only one way out of this," Joe joked. "Martin, we're going to have to kill you."

The elevator opened on the third floor, and Martin and the Hardys stepped out. "I'm right over here," Martin said, moving to the room opposite the elevator.

Joe turned back for a final glimpse of the blond girls. They giggled and waved as the door slid shut. "Nice town," Joe told Martin. "I'm definitely going to like it here."

"Wait till you get to know it," Martin said. "Tomorrow we'll meet at eight o'clock in the lobby. We'll have breakfast and then we'll begin the tour. I'll leave you on your own about noon. The car and driver are yours to use for the next couple of days. Go anywhere you want."

"Great," Frank said, glancing at his key. "Which way's three-thirteen?"

Martin pointed to the left. The Hardys headed for a bend in the hallway. "Remember, eight sharp," he called after them. Then they were gone.

Martin closed his door and crossed the room to a large window, opening it wide. He stood for a moment, inhaling the sea air. Then he moved back to a small desk. On top of it were a handful of pens and a ream of writing paper in a large wooden box. Martin pulled the paper from the box and set it to one side.

Hidden in the bottom of the box was a compact shortwave radio. Martin put on the earphone and picked up a small mike. He touched a switch on its side and raised it to his lips.

"The couriers are now in place," he said into the microphone. "Tomorrow's rendezvous will go as planned."

"Plans change," said an unfamiliar, accented voice behind him.

Startled, Martin turned and stared for a second at his attacker. Something hard cracked against his temple. The mike slipped from his fingers. And then he slowly toppled to the floor.

Chapter

2

FRANK HARDY LOOKED at his watch and frowned. It was seven past eight the next morning, and he was eager to begin the tour of the city. Instead, he was sitting on a couch in the hotel lobby, rhythmically tapping his fingers on the arm as he watched the stairs, waiting for Martin to appear. Joe sat across the lobby, watching the elevator. But there was no sign of their guide.

The minutes ticked by. By a quarter past eight Joe walked over to Frank and said, "He's not coming."

"Why?" Frank asked. "Do you think he missed his wake-up call?"

"He sure missed mine," said Joe. "I rang his room five minutes ago. No answer. Maybe he

11

went out last night to check some of those discos he talked about. I bet he's dead to the world."

Frank heard his brother's stomach growl, and the sound made him smile. "Just a minute," he said, and walked over to the hotel desk. After a few words with the man behind the desk, he returned to Joe.

"What was that all about?" Joe asked.

"Breakfast," Frank replied. "The desk clerk says there's a little café around the corner. I left word for Martin to meet us there."

"Think he'll mind if we start without him?"

Frank glanced again at the empty stairs and then at his watch. Eight twenty-five. "He knows where to find us—and I feel like having more than a hotel breakfast."

"Great," Joe said. "Let's go."

They stepped outside and walked down the narrow street to the corner. On the other side of the street was their limousine, the driver leaning against it with a newspaper in his hands. Dark glasses still hid his eyes. And from the angle he held the paper, Frank wasn't sure if he was reading or watching the street. Either way, he never moved.

The Hardys went into the café, and soon a waiter brought a tray of sausages, toast, and oranges and set it in front of them.

"Let's hit the beach this afternoon," Joe said after finishing an orange.

"Mmmm?" Frank said, his mouth full of toast.

"When the tour's over. We've got the afternoon free, remember?" Joe held up a hand and studied his skin. "I've got to work on my tan."

"And the girls," Frank said.

"And the girls," Joe admitted, laughing as he called the waiter over. He got the bill, dug a handful of Spanish pesetas from his pocket, and dropped them on the table.

The sun had already made the city hot. It was cooled only by an occasional ocean breeze. The street was busy, clogged with cars in the road and pedestrians on the sidewalk. Despite the antiquity of many of the buildings, Málaga was as modern as any city.

Which is what Martin would tell us, Frank thought. If he were here.

As they passed their car, the driver waved at them and then crossed the street. He drew a long white envelope from his pocket and handed it to Frank without a word.

"It's from Martin," Frank said after tearing the envelope open. He had several sheets of paper with typing on them. The top sheet read:

Dear Frank and Joe,
    Sorry I can't be with you this morning. Continue without me. The driver knows where to take you. Good luck.

                                        Martin

Under the first sheet were more papers, detailing the tour and the special features and history of the places they were scheduled to see. "Does this mean we can go straight to the beach?" Joe asked.

"We've got the car for only a couple of days," Frank said, slipping the notes into his shirt pocket. "Plenty of time for the beach later. Let's go see the town while we can."

"Can we get a new driver?" Joe whispered as they crossed the street. "This one's not my choice for tour guide of the year. He looks like his face will fall off if he smiles."

"I know what you mean," Frank whispered. The driver opened the back door for them. Frank and Joe slid in. "He doesn't smile, he doesn't talk, and I still haven't gotten a good look at his face," he said so only Joe could hear. The door slammed behind him. "But think of it this way: Who looks a gift horse in the mouth?"

The driver got in and turned on the ignition. The limousine roared to life, then pulled into the traffic. In seconds the Hardys found themselves swept along through the streets of Málaga.

As they neared the city's waterfront, traffic thinned out, and the car cruised the Paseo del Parque beside the harbor. "Look," Joe said, pointing at the palm-shaded walkways that lined the marina. "It looks like California."

"But there's something you won't see in California," said Frank, reading the tour notes. He pointed to an ancient limestone church crowned by two towers. "That cathedral dates back to the sixteenth century."

To Frank's surprise, the limousine drove right past the cathedral and turned a corner, heading back to the center of town. "Hey!" shouted Frank. "We were supposed to stop there!"

"No time," said the driver, his voice a harsh whisper.

"What do you know?" Joe said. "He talks."

"Great." Frank gave the driver a sour look, then studied the notes again as the car traveled the Málaga streets. "Can you see where we are now?"

Joe craned his neck. "The Plaza de la Merced. Any idea what that is?"

The limousine screeched to a halt at the curb. "Thirty minutes," the driver muttered.

"This isn't exactly the tour I had in mind," Joe said as they climbed out of the car.

Frank pocketed the notes. "According to Martin, the birthplace of Pablo Picasso is right near here. Let's go find it."

Joe shrugged, and together they crossed to the far side of the plaza. After a short walk they found a small building. Like many other buildings they had seen, this one had old wooden shutters on its windows and small balconies on every floor. A small sign was tacked up next to the door, and among the Spanish words was the name Pablo Picasso.

"This must be it," Frank said. "You'd think it would be a lot less ordinary looking, wouldn't you?" He squinted at the notice. "I wonder what this says."

Joe gently nudged his brother aside. "Let an expert translate. I've been waiting to try my high school Spanish."

"A memorial is to be erected here to commemorate the birth of the great artist Pablo Picasso," said a soft voice behind them. "This will become an official historical site."

The Hardys turned. And Joe smiled. A pretty young Spanish woman, dressed in a print blouse and denim skirt, was standing and staring at them with large brown eyes.

"Thank you," Frank said. He held out his hand. "I'm Frank Hardy, and this is my brother, Joe. We're Americans."

The woman's eyes narrowed, and she made no move to shake Frank's hand. "The sky is bluer in Barcelona," she said.

"That's very interesting," Frank replied.

"The sky is bluer in Barcelona," she repeated, tension sounding in her voice.

The smile faded from Joe's lips, and he looked bewildered. "Want to get something to drink, Frank?"

"Sounds like a good idea," Frank answered.

To the girl he said, "Thanks again for your help." Before she could react, the Hardys moved away from her.

"The sky is bluer in Barcelona!" she shouted desperately, but they were already halfway across the plaza. Curious stares from passersby silenced her.

"What was that about?" Frank wondered aloud. "It almost sounded like some sort of code."

"Beats me," Joe said. "Nice looking, but—" He shook his head and sighed. "Why do I always run into crazy ones?" Wistfully, he glanced over his shoulder for a last look at her.

At first he thought she was waving. Then he realized she was pointing. That's when he saw a man, dressed in a dark suit and sunglasses, step from a doorway.

As he looked around, he saw three similar men moving into position all around the Plaza de la Merced. They were all closing in on the Hardys.

"We've got trouble," Joe yelled. "Head for the limo. Quick!"

Frank nodded and broke into a sprint. In seconds they had reached their car and scrambled into the back seat. The four men were only yards away. "Windows up," Frank ordered. He pressed the button on the window control, but nothing moved. "Driver!" he called. "Get us out of—"

He stopped. Their driver wasn't in the car.

"Are the keys in the ignition?" Frank asked Joe. He glanced out the window. The four men were closing in.

"Nope," Joe replied, leaning over the front seat. His hand scooped down and came back up with a false beard and latex nose in it. "But I found *part* of our driver."

"A disguise?" Frank's bewilderment changed to anger. "We've been set up!"

A hand thrust through the open car window. In it was a small-caliber pistol. Frank looked up to see a man in sunglasses grinning unpleasantly at him. The man's three companions stood around the car, each guarding one door. Another limousine, with a diplomatic license plate, appeared from around the corner.

In a thick Russian accent the gunman said, "You are to be coming with us. Now."

"Any idea of what's going on?" Joe asked Frank as the men outside began to pull open the doors.

"I'm not sure," Frank said, "but I have this weird notion we're being kidnapped by the KGB!"

Chapter

3

"The KGB?" said Joe. "Well, I hope they get a real kick out of *this*." He slammed his heel into the unlocked car door, smashing it open. It struck the man outside, knocking him backward into the gunman behind him.

Joe barreled out of the car.

The man standing outside Frank's door raised his gun. Instantly, Frank drove his fist through the open window and into the man's stomach. Caught off guard, the Russian doubled over.

The fourth man swung his pistol toward Frank, but it was too late. Frank caught his wrist and hauled up. The man flew into the car, banging his head against the roof. As he fell away, Frank swung his door open, leaping out of the car.

"This way!" Joe shouted, and Frank followed

him toward the corner of the block. Already, the Russians were recovering, and Frank knew they'd be after them in seconds.

"I think we can lose them," Frank told his brother as they ran down a narrow street. Just ahead was a busy intersection. The traffic made it almost impossible to cross. "If we can just get to the other side—"

He scanned the intersection for a break in the traffic, but there was none. The rapid footsteps behind them raced closer, and Frank could hear words muttered in Russian. There was no time to wait, he knew. They had to make their move now.

He hurled himself into traffic. Tires screeched and horns blared as drivers slammed on their brakes. *"Turistas locos!"* someone yelled, and others joined in. Frank ignored them, focusing on nothing but the other side of the street. Out of the corner of his eye he could see Joe keeping pace with him.

At last they jumped over the far curb. "Made it," Frank said breathlessly.

"Keep running," he told Joe, and both broke into a sprint again. Their gamble hadn't worked too well for them. Traffic had now ground to a stop, and the Russians were crossing the street with ease.

The Hardys reached an alley. Ducking into it, they slowed down. The alley was damp and littered with piles of garbage, and the buildings it ran between were close enough together to shade it from the sun. "Shhh," Frank said. "I'm pretty sure they didn't see us come in. If we're quiet, they might pass by."

As Frank spoke, the Russians appeared at the end of the alley. Frank and Joe crouched against a wall, dropping out of sight behind a garbage pile. Cautiously, they peered over the top of the garbage. They hadn't been spotted.

The four Russians were standing on the street, arguing. One pointed into the alley and another pointed down the street. Finally, two of them went down the street.

The other two drew their guns and stepped warily into the alley, slowly moving toward the Hardys. One of the Russians kicked at a garbage pile, scattering it everywhere. He shook his head at his partner, and they cautiously moved closer.

"They must think we're hiding in the garbage," Frank whispered to Joe. "They underestimated us at the car, but I doubt that's going to happen again."

"Let's make it happen," Joe whispered back. As the shadow of a gun fell over his face, he dug into the garbage and flung it into the air. Instinctively, the Russians spun and took aim at the flying rubbish.

Joe rushed between them, catching each of them around the waist with an arm and forcing them back against a wall. Before they could react, Joe threw a punch at the Russian to his left. The man toppled to the ground.

As he whirled to deal with the other one, Joe felt the sharp smack of metal against his temple, and he staggered back, pain exploding behind his eyes. Through the haze he could see the Russian's gun. It was what had hit his head, he knew, and now it was aimed at his chest.

"Hiii-ya!" Frank shouted, and his foot lashed out, kicking the gun from the startled Russian's hand. The heel of Frank's hand smashed into the Russian's jaw, and the man dropped.

Joe rubbed his head, clearing his vision. "Two down, two to go," he said. They ran for the far end of the alley.

"I'd rather we didn't meet the other two again at all," Frank replied. "Let's try to get back to the hotel."

"Do you hear something?" Joe asked.

Frank listened. Circus music, but distorted, he thought. Tinny, like guitar music. He didn't know what it could be.

The alley opened into the back of a church-yard. "Through here. It'll be quicker," Joe said, and they entered the church. Its high, domed ceiling was painted with angels. Set into the walls were wooden statues of saints.

Frank pulled open the front door of the church, and he and Joe froze.

In the street in front of the church was a parade. The sidewalks were lined with spectators. *"Buenos días,"* said a voice behind them.

They turned. A priest stood in the aisle, dressed in a traditional black cassock. He smiled at them and said, "Every year we have a street festival at this time. Come! You are welcome to join us."

With a slight bow he closed the doors of the church and led them down the steps to the street. Halfway down, Joe nudged Frank in the ribs.

"Look," Joe said, nodding toward the street.

Frank peered through the crowd, and his heart sank. Across the street, on the other side of the parade, were the other two Russians. They were watching them.

"Keep going," Frank told Joe. "They won't try anything with this many people around, and it'll be easy to lose them in the crowd."

They left the priest and started walking beside the parade. Frank could see the Russians on the other side keeping pace with them. But the brightly dressed marchers and rows of carts pulled by oxen and decorated with streamers and flowers kept the Russians from crossing the street.

"That keeps them in *their* place," Joe said, laughing. "They'll never get to us."

"We have to go to them sooner or later. Our

hotel is in that direction. We'll have to cross over.''

A squad of musicians, mostly drummers, followed the lines of carts. Frank stared down the length of the marchers until he saw the end of the street. "It looks like the parade's coming to another plaza. Maybe we can get across there."

On the other side of the street, the Russians shadowed them step for step.

At the plaza, people in traditional Spanish costumes danced on the pavement. Women in long, full dresses, flowers in their hair, twirled arm in arm with men in short vests, white shirts, and tight black slacks.

As the Hardys were passing them, the dancers went into the crowd and pulled spectators into the dance with them.

"This way," Frank told Joe. "I have an idea."

The Hardys skirted the circle of dancers, watching the Russians move around on the other side.

"Now," Frank said, and he stuck out a hand. A woman caught it and tugged him into the circle. Almost before he knew what was happening, Frank was passed from woman to woman. Dizzy from the spinning, he kept his eye on the Russians as he drew nearer and nearer to them with each step. Behind him, Joe was also dancing, waiting for Frank's next move.

As he passed the first Russian, Frank grabbed

the man's wrist and pulled him into the dance, handing him to the next woman in the circle. The woman laughed and pulled the Russian along, and Frank stepped out of the dance and into the crowd.

The last man turned to reach for Frank, but Joe caught the man's arm and repeated his brother's trick.

"Run," Frank said, pushing through the crowd. Joe followed, laughing as he thought of the Russians caught among the dancers.

They reached the open street and ran. When they had run several blocks, cutting from street to street, they stopped to catch their breath. No one was following them. "We finally lost them," Frank said. "I figured they'd want to keep a low profile and not cause a scene around the locals. That gave us the edge we needed."

"We'd better not run into those guys again," Joe replied. "I think we're all out of edges. I can't wait to get my hands on Martin and find out what this is all about."

"You think he had something to do with it?"

"He vanishes, our chauffeur does a disappearing act, and suddenly there are goons crawling all over us," Joe said. "Hey, he was supposed to be with us today. Maybe they weren't after us—maybe they were looking for Martin."

"There's only one way to find out." Frank

glanced around one last time but saw no sign of the Russians. "Let's get back to the hotel."

They entered the hotel through the back door and climbed the back stairs to the third floor. The walk back had been long and difficult.

"If you want to go to our room, I'll bring Martin around," Joe suggested. "We'll meet you there."

"Fine," Frank said. "He's got a lot of explaining to do." He left Joe and turned the corner, walking down the corridor to their room.

Frank stopped, ducking into a doorway. A policeman was standing in front of their doors. Frank slipped along the corridor, heading back to the stairs.

Joe was waiting, a look of dread on his face. "Frank," he said, "there's a cop in front of Martin's door, and a sign on it saying only police are allowed to enter. What's going on?"

"I don't know," Frank replied. "But we're in the thick of it. The cops are watching our room too." He started down the stairs. "Maybe we can find something out from the front desk."

"Looks like rush hour, doesn't it?" Joe said as they reached the main floor. Dozens of people, guests at the hotel, milled around the lobby. Scattered among them were policemen handing out photographs. Near the front desk were two pretty blondes. "Those are the girls who were on the elevator last night. Maybe they've heard something. Let's go ask—" He started moving toward them.

Frank pulled him back, around a pillar. "Let's not," Frank said. "Look who they're talking to."

Joe peered around the pillar. The young women were speaking to a tall, burly man with dark hair. He wore a dark tailored suit and tie. He nodded, recording the girls' words in a small notebook.

"Cop?" Joe asked Frank.

"Plainclothes," Frank answered. "He's probably the one running the show here."

"Let's go talk to him, then," Joe said, and started around the pillar. The man with the notebook had closed it and turned to the desk clerk.

The man spoke to the clerk in a deep voice that cut through the din. *"Hermanos,"* Joe heard the Spanish word for "brothers." He strained to catch more, and was lucky. The policeman spoke clearly and slowly. He was easy to understand. "They were seen with the man just before the time of death, and were heard making threats against him."

The anxious clerk spoke quickly, but Joe caught something about murder being bad for the hotel.

"It will be over soon," the dark-haired policeman said, "when I arrest Frank and Joseph Hardy for the murder of Martin Chase."

Chapter

4

JOE DUCKED BACK behind the pillar. "Big trouble, Frank," he said. "We've got to get out of here."

Frank glanced over his shoulder at the back door, but it was no longer unguarded. A policeman stood there, checking the tourists who came in. "If we go, we go out the front," Frank muttered. He scanned the lobby. The other guests were chatting with one another, acting as if a party were going on. On the wall to the Hardys' left was a small newsstand. "Follow me," Frank said. "If we act naturally and don't attract any attention, we should be able to pull this off."

Casually, he strolled over to the kiosk, picked out a paper, and handed some coins to the vendor. Frank opened the paper, folding back a page and holding it up so that it blocked the lower half of his face. He turned to face the room.

No one noticed him. The policeman in the dark suit was speaking to the young blond women again. And next to them a uniformed policeman worked on a sketch. He's drawing us from their descriptions, Frank thought. The police will have pictures of us in no time.

Behind the cover of the paper Frank jerked his head to one side, signaling Joe to make his move. Then Frank began to walk, apparently aimlessly, toward the front door, flipping through his newspaper like a tourist looking for somewhere to go.

Frank walked through the front door and onto the street and breathed a sigh of relief. He tossed the newspaper into a trash basket. Where was Joe? he wondered. Had they finished the sketch and recognized him before he could escape?

No, there was Joe, coming out the door.

"Now what?" Joe asked, joining him in front of the hotel. "All our stuff is in our room, and we can't get to it. What are we going to do?"

Before Frank could answer, a cry of *"Alto!"* sounded behind them. They turned to see a uniformed policeman with a paper in hand. He spoke to them rapidly in Spanish.

He's got us, Frank thought. That must be our picture in his hand. As if hearing Frank's thoughts, the policeman thrust the paper into

29

their faces and started asking more questions in Spanish.

The picture he held was a photograph of Martin.

"He wants to know if we know the man in the picture," Joe said, and then, to the policeman, *"No. Dispenseme. No comprendo."*

The policeman nodded, shrugged his shoulders, then went back toward the hotel.

"Come on," Frank said. "Let's hit that café where we had breakfast. We can rest and sort things out there."

The Hardys entered the café and sat at a back table that was partially hidden by lush green plants. Seconds later a waiter appeared with menus. It was the same waiter who had served them at breakfast, and his lean face brightened when he recognized them.

"You are back," he said slowly in English. "I am Francisco. What may I bring you, my friends?"

"Dos Coca-Colas, por favor," Joe answered.

The waiter spun around and vanished into the kitchen.

"He sure is friendly," Joe said, grinning. "I must have tipped him better than I thought."

"Great." Frank rubbed his eyes tiredly. "Someone else who can recognize us." He looked around the room. Besides the door they had come in through, there was a door to the kitchen. Good, we can reach that easily if we have to, Frank thought. "Why are the cops looking for us anyway?"

Joe stared at his brother. "I thought you heard. They think we killed Martin."

"What?" Frank looked angry. "Where did they get *that* idea?"

"How should I know?" Joe said. "Maybe we should turn ourselves in. After all, we *are* innocent."

"I don't think so," Frank responded. "This whole thing is starting to smell like a setup. If someone fingered us for Martin's murder, who knows what evidence they've manufactured? We're not in America, Joe. I have a feeling we'd better be able to *prove* our innocence before we start talking to any police."

Francisco reappeared with the drinks. "Mind if we sit here a bit?" Frank asked. "We'll order some food in a little while."

"*Sí!*" the waiter said, flashing his smile at them. "Stay as long as you like. Eat! Eat!" He wandered toward the front of the restaurant.

Sure that they were alone again, Joe sipped his drink and said, "You've got a point. We're probably better off on the streets." He chuckled. "Besides, we don't want to make it too easy for the Russians to find us, do we? You don't suppose *they* set us up?"

Frank shook his head. "There wasn't time.

31

You know who I bet could give us a few answers? Our chauffeur. He's the one who gave us Martin's note. And he led us to the Russians. Maybe he's working for them—at least, his disappearance was awfully well-timed."

"You're right," Joe agreed. "But we don't even know what he looks like. I never got a good look at his face, and his face wasn't his real face anyway. He could be anyone."

"We can't even be sure he's a he," Frank said. "It could possibly have been a woman."

Joe's eyes widened. "You don't suppose that Spanish girl at the plaza . . ."

"I doubt it," Frank said with a shrug. "Too slight. The chauffeur's height and build would be hard to fake. No, I'd guess he was a man. I wish he'd had a scar, some peculiar mannerism, *something* we could identify him with."

"We're not finding him unless he wants to be found," Joe said. "And we can't walk up to the Russians and ask them what's going on. I don't see any way we can help ourselves until we get a handle on the situation."

Suddenly Frank snapped his fingers and said excitedly, "There's *one* person who might be able to clue us in!"

"Who?" Joe asked. "The girl?"

A broad grin spread across Frank's face. "Martin."

"Martin? But he's—"

Frank waved a finger, cutting off his brother's thought. "Right. But the police have sealed off his room, so odds are everything he had is still in there."

"Of course!" Joe said. "If he left any information in his room—but how do we get in?"

"That's what we've got to figure out," Frank replied. "One thing's for sure. We'll have to wait until dark. Till then, we might as well eat." He picked up the menu and studied it, then raised his hand to flag the waiter to the table.

Despite the bright spotlights that lit up the front of the hotel at night, the rear of the place was dark, except for the parking-lot lights and ground lamps that marked the edges of walkways.

Frank and Joe slipped around to the back of the hotel, staying in the shadows. There were no signs of police in the parking lot, and guests were coming and going now as they pleased.

"I don't know if we should have spent so much time in that café," Joe whispered. "All that food is starting to weigh me down." A car sped by them, catching them in its headlights, and the boys turned their heads to hide their faces.

"We can make up for it by eating light for the rest of the trip," Frank answered. "Besides, if this doesn't work, we may not get another chance to eat at all. Did you leave a big tip?"

"Sure. Never know when we'll have to hide out there for a few hours again."

Following his brother, Joe crouched down and darted across the parking lot until he reached the safety of the darkness on the other side. Now they were at the bushes just in back of their hotel, and he looked up to the third floor, counting silently to himself. "There's our room," he said, pointing to a window on the third floor. "Four rooms in from the end."

Frank nodded. "That's good to know for when we have to get in there."

Joe walked to the corner of the building and turned up the side, counting carefully. Finally he stopped under two balconies, one above the other, and looked up. The top balcony was dark, and he could see no shadows on the shades drawn inside the room there. "Martin's."

Frank cupped his hands together and held them down at his knees, palms up. "Ready?" he asked Joe.

"Ready," Joe said. He broke into a sprint, heading straight for Frank. His last step landed in Frank's cupped hands, and Frank jerked upward, hurling Joe into the air. Joe stretched out his arms, and his fingers locked onto the balcony above him. Straining, he pulled himself up and over the railing and rolled with a thud onto the balcony.

Joe flattened himself on the balcony floor and

reached down through the railing until Frank gripped his hand. "Hold on," Joe said. Slowly, he lifted his brother up. Finally, Frank grabbed the bottom of a rail and dragged himself onto the balcony.

"One down," Frank said breathlessly. "Care to try for another?"

"Why not?" Joe said, gathering his strength. Frank cupped his hands together again, and in seconds Joe had disappeared over the railing of the top balcony.

For a long minute Frank watched in vain for some sign of him. But there wasn't even a sound.

"Joe!" he whispered. "Are you all right?"

As if in answer, an arm extended down from the top balcony. Frank grabbed it and hung on as he was lifted.

"You know, you could have answered me," Frank complained as he came over the railing. "I thought something had hap—"

That's when he realized Joe wasn't alone. Two policemen were holding his arms. Standing in front of Frank was the man who had been interviewing the blond girls that afternoon.

"You are Frank Hardy?" the man asked in accented English. "I've been waiting to meet you. I am Police Inspector Melendez.

"You and your brother are under arrest."

Chapter

5

"YOU CAN'T ARREST US," Joe said. "We haven't done anything."

Police Inspector Melendez clutched Frank's arm and shoved him inside the room beside Joe. "Sit down," he said. The Hardys sat on the bed. "Men who haven't done anything don't come creeping into dead men's rooms through the balcony in the middle of the night. Perhaps in America murder is considered nothing—"

"That's not what I meant," Joe interrupted.

"But in Spain we take it very seriously," Inspector Melendez continued as if Joe had said nothing. "What was your relationship with the dead man?"

"You mean Martin?" Frank said. "We met him only once, yesterday. He was supposed to be our guide around Málaga. I'd won this contest—"

Inspector Melendez cut him off. "Then what was your motive for killing him?"

"You're crazy if you think we did it," Joe said.

Inspector Melendez scowled. "I would be crazy to think you did not. You were the last persons to be seen with him before his death and the only persons ever seen with him in this hotel."

"What about the chauffeur?" Frank asked.

"Chauffeur?" Inspector Melendez repeated. He pulled out his notebook and leafed through it. "No one else has mentioned a chauffeur. Please describe him."

Frank swallowed hard. "We can't. He had disguised his face."

"I see." With a sigh of exasperation Inspector Melendez flipped the notebook closed and returned it to his pocket. "You were overheard to threaten Martin Chase in the elevator."

"That was a joke," Joe said. "A figure of speech."

"And we have this," Inspector Melendez replied. With a tweezers he held up a piece of writing paper. On it were bloodstains and three handwritten words: "Frank and Joe." "The dead man's handwriting. The paper is covered with his fingerprints. The pen that wrote those words was in his hand when he was found."

"None of that proves anything," Frank said.

"Perhaps," Inspector Melendez replied. "I think he was trying to name his killers but never got the chance to finish. Have you another explanation?"

Joe started to stand, but a policeman put a hand on his shoulder, forcing him to sit. "He could have been leaving us a note."

"With his dying breath?" Inspector Melendez said. "I find that unlikely."

"All right. A warning then."

The inspector dropped his cigarette to the floor, ground it out with his heel, and looked at Joe with new interest. "Oh? Of what would he need to warn you?"

He'll never believe us, Frank thought. Everything we say just makes us better suspects. "We were chased by Russians this morning and spent all day trying to stay out of their way," he said in a weary voice. "He might have been trying to tell us about them."

With a burst of laughter Inspector Melendez asked, "Russians? You are spies, then?"

"No, but—" Frank began.

"Then what," the inspector continued, "would Russians want with you?"

The Hardys looked at each other. Their last card was played, and it was useless. They were beaten.

"We don't know," Joe said.

Inspector Melendez snapped his fingers, and

the two policemen stood up straight. One grasped Joe's shoulder and the other took hold of Frank. "One last thing," Inspector Melendez asked. "What did you expect to find here?"

Joe shook his head. "Something to prove our innocence, I guess."

"Take them to headquarters," Melendez ordered. "We will get some *real* answers from them there." The policemen shoved Frank and Joe to the door of the room.

The whole situation was hopeless. No one would believe their story—unless *they* did something to prove it. Frank glanced at the door, and Joe nodded. As they were going through the door, Frank said, "Now!"

Together they spun, and each shoved one of the policemen back into the room. "Run," Frank shouted, and together they headed for the front stairs.

Next to the stairs the elevator had stopped and was letting people out. Behind them Frank could hear Inspector Melendez and the policemen coming out of Martin's room. Inspector Melendez yelled in Spanish, and Joe could hear a pistol cock.

"The elevator!" Joe said. "They won't shoot while there are other people around." He pushed through the crowd coming off the elevator and grabbed the door, holding it open. A second later Frank jumped into the car, and Joe let the door slip closed. As the elevator sank in its shaft, Joe could see Inspector Melendez furiously ordering his man down the stairs.

On the main floor the elevator door slid open. The Hardys raced across the lobby with Inspector Melendez and his men only a few yards behind them. "Outside!" Frank said. "We'll lose them in the dark."

But as they stepped through the door, they were greeted by the glare of the lights that lit the front of the building. "We're better targets out here than in there," Joe said reasonably. Three steps at a time, they sped down the front steps to the relative darkness of the street.

They were halfway across the street when a dark van screeched to a halt between them and the police. Before Joe or Frank could react, the side door of the van was slid open and strong arms gripped them, dragging them inside. A damp cloth pressed against Joe's face, and the stench of chloroform burned into his nose and mouth, filling his lungs. The last things he saw before plunging into unconsciousness were his now sleeping brother and the face of the girl who had spoken to them at Picasso's birthplace.

A coarse cloth patted Joe's cheek, and he tried to open his eyes. "Frank?" he called out. "Are you there?"

"Your brother is here," said a rough, cold

voice, and Joe's eyes snapped open. Sunlight glared into them, and he raised a hand to shield his face. There were bars on the windows of the room. He rolled his head to see Frank seated on a chair a few feet away. Another chair stood in front of him. Except for a small table with a lamp on it, the rest of the room was bare.

Morning, he realized. He remembered the police and the van and the sting of chloroform fumes. Captured, he thought. But who?

The girl from the plaza knelt beside him, a cloth in her hands. "Are you all right?" she asked, with genuine concern in her voice.

"Silence, Elena! Move away from the boy," ordered the cold voice. The girl backed off. Joe stared up at a bald man with a heavyset build. Standing behind him, one on either side of the door, were two of the Russians who had chased them across Málaga the day before. The bald man scowled at Joe impatiently. "Tell me the name."

Joe looked at Frank. "KGB?"

Frank nodded. "His name's Vladimir. The boss, I guess. He keeps asking about some name."

The man called Vladimir gave them a frosty smile. "The Network should not employ babbling children."

Joe stiffened. He and Frank had worked with the supersecret government agency called the Network in the past. But there had been no

41

contact between them for several months. Now, it seemed, the Network was back to haunt them.

"What network are you talking about? NBC?" Frank said. "And who are you calling children?"

"Do not play the fool." Vladimir's voice was cold and flat, but his eyes glittered with menace. "You will not get your agent back until we have received the name. We had an agreement, your masters and mine."

"I'm starting to get it," Frank said to Joe. "The *Network* set us up. I gather Martin was working for them—"

"Of course he was," Vladimir told them impatiently. "Just as you are. He reported he had passed the name to you. And now I want it."

"The Network pulled a fast one on you, pal," Joe said. "We've got nothing to do with them."

"Ah." Vladimir shrugged and turned away. Then he pivoted, throwing his weight into a slap aimed at Joe's face. But it never connected. Instinctively, Joe reached up and blocked the blow. Then he clenched his fist and drew back his arm. At the door safeties clicked off two pistols.

"No!" shouted Elena. She flung herself between Vladimir and Joe, pushing them apart. To Vladimir she said, "You promised it would not be like this." Then to Joe she whispered, "Strike him and they will shoot you."

Vladimir shoved her away. "They will cooperate—or suffer." He pushed Joe off his chair. "I

42

would think carefully,'' Vladimir said as he grasped Joe's arm and tossed him back in the chair. "Your only hope of leaving this consulate alive is to give me answers."

Joe shook his head and said nothing.

Vladimir shrugged. "Perhaps they don't believe me." He went to the gunmen by the door and took one of their pistols. "We do not need both of them. If this one will not cooperate, perhaps his death will convince the other one." He sighted along the barrel, aiming at Joe's head.

"Don't move now." Smiling at his little joke, he slowly squeezed the trigger.

A black-gloved hand reached in the door and seized Vladimir's wrist, jerking his hand back and up. The bald man whirled around, furious, then he jerked back in surprise. "Konstantin!"

Whoever this Konstantin might be, it was obvious that Vladimir wasn't expecting him and wasn't happy to see him. The tall blond stranger, on the other hand, was calm and completely at ease. His piercing blue eyes twinkled over his confident smile.

"Vladimir, Vladimir," Konstantin said as he took the gun away. "Exile to this lonely country has not changed your ways?"

Vladimir rubbed his bruised wrist, still glaring. "What brings you to Spain, comrade?" he asked. "Have you come to invite me back to Department V?"

"Department V?" Frank whispered to Joe. "That's the KGB's assassination bureau!"

"No, Vladimir." Konstantin put a restraining hand on the big man's shoulder as he studied the Hardys. "The department is no secret—not among *professionals*." He emphasized the word as Vladimir's eyes narrowed angrily. "However, we prefer stealth and skill, not the brute force you demonstrate here."

Furious, Vladimir shrugged off Konstantin's hand and headed for the door. "Very well, I leave them in *your* hands. We shall see whose methods are most effective." He turned on his heel and stormed off, slamming the door behind him.

Sighing with relief, Elena picked herself up off the floor and approached Konstantin. "Thank goodness you arrived when you did, comrade. He was about to torture them, I'm sure."

Konstantin shook his head. "How terrible. Brutality solves nothing. There are more appropriate techniques." Casually, he walked to the table, picked up the lamp, and ripped the wire from its base. The lamp cord, still plugged into the wall, sprayed a shower of sparks as the exposed wires met.

With the look of a scientist who has performed the same experiment many times, he moved the sparking wires toward Joe's face. "Now," he said, "we shall get our answers."

Chapter
6

"DON'T!" ELENA SCREAMED. "How can you think of such a thing? Who *are* you?"

Konstantin blinked at Elena as if noticing her for the first time. To one of the gunmen he said, "One of ours?" The gunman shook his head, and Konstantin faced Elena again. "Ah! One of Vladimir's local puppets. This is beyond you, girl."

"You can't—" she began, but Konstantin cut her off.

"I *can*. I am Vladimir's superior. While he may permit you to question his decisions, I will not. Perhaps your loyalty to the Party is insincere—"

"I am loyal," Elena insisted. "But torture—"

"This is incentive," he said, tapping the live wires together, creating a fat spark.

"You don't need that wire," Frank told him. "We've been telling the truth."

Nodding, Konstantin rested the cord on the table so that the ends dangled off without touching. "But one must make certain, no? Let us put together a picture of events.

"One: My government graciously accepted a proposal from your agency to exchange a captured agent for a piece of information of extreme interest to us. Your agent had been caught in the midst of treacherous action against the Soviet Union."

"Agency?" Joe asked. "You're talking about the Network?"

"Two: You were chosen as couriers to deliver this information to us. Your own contact radioed that you had received it. Yet, when *our* go-between"—he waved a thumb at Elena—"contacted you, you refused to speak with her or turn over the information. I wish to know why."

"We still don't know what you're talking about." Frank sighed.

Konstantin shrugged and lifted the cord from the table. "So you say."

"Perhaps," Elena said uncertainly, "they *are* telling the truth."

"And perhaps *you* betrayed us. You could have ruined the exchange." Konstantin turned toward Elena, the sparking wires in his hand now pointing at her.

Elena backed away in horror, fiercely shaking her head.

Konstantin turned away from her, disgusted. "Get the fool out of here." One of the guards stepped forward and grasped Elena's shoulder. He shoved her toward the door.

"Leave her alone!" Joe shouted. Without thinking, he leapt from his chair, fists clenched. The gunman released Elena, and he and his partner spun, their pistols out and aimed at Joe.

With a shriek Elena threw herself against the gunman next to her, knocking him off balance. As he stumbled, her hand snaked out, and before Konstantin or the other guard could move, the pistol was in her hands.

"Now let them go!" she ordered.

Konstantin set the cord down again. "You are free to leave," he told Frank and Joe.

The second gunman lunged for Elena, but she pivoted and aimed at him. He stood flat-footed and scowled. "Your gun," Elena said to the man. "Give it to him." She pointed to Joe.

Konstantin sat casually on the edge of the table and joined his hands behind his head.

"Let's go," Frank said.

Konstantin smiled and shook his head. "You may leave this room, but you will not escape the consulate."

"We'll see," Frank said as Joe and Elena slipped from the room. He joined them in the hallway a second later, then slipped the outside bolt on the door, locking Konstantin and the gunmen in the room.

The long hallway was lined with doors, and they were at the end of it. At the other end was a stairway. "Any other way out?" Joe asked Elena.

She shook her head sadly. "No. There are three floors below us. I am sorry. This is all my fault."

"We'll discuss that later," Frank said, taking the gun from Elena and pocketing it. "We've got to get out of here before they sound the alarm." They ran for the stairs. "How many people does Vladimir have in here?"

"I don't know," Elena said. "A dozen, two dozen perhaps. It is the Soviet consulate. I'm sorry."

"Oh, great," Frank said.

A Russian voice shouted from the stairs they were running toward. A guard stood staring at them. He pulled back the bolt on his AK47 assault rifle.

A stream of bullets from that, the Hardys knew, would cut them in half before they could even reach the Russian—and the guard looked only too eager to shoot.

Joe shrugged, took the pistol he carried by its barrel, and started to raise his hands.

The Russian grinned—then stared in confusion

as Joe's hand kept going up, hurling the pistol at the guard's head.

"Down!" Joe warned, falling to the floor as Frank tackled Elena.

The hurtling pistol caught the Russian in the head. He tumbled forward, riddling the ceiling with bullets before he collapsed.

"Joe," Elena cried. Her eyes brightened as he got to his feet. "I thought you were—"

"I'm okay," Joe answered, flashing her a smile. He picked up the AK47.

They heard heavy boots pounding up the stairs toward them. "This way!" Elena said. She flung open one of the many heavy oak doors. They dashed inside and she slammed it behind them, slipping the locks into place.

"Where are we?" Frank asked. The room was paneled in dark wood. One wall was lined with bookshelves while the opposite wall was lined with file cabinets.

"Vladimir's private office," Elena said as someone began pounding on the other side of the door. "He is very concerned with security. The door will hold."

"It's only a matter of time before someone shows up with the key."

"There is only one duplicate," Elena said.

Joe looked over the room, stopping at a glass door set in the wall. Behind the door was a fire extinguisher, hose, and ax. "Get a load of this."

Frank pulled open a file drawer and started rifling the files. "Let's see what he keeps in this. Any way out of here, Joe?"

"Maybe." Joe drew aside the thick curtains covering the windows and rapped on the glass with his knuckles. "Bulletproof. A cautious guy, this Vladimir." Joe looked out the window and smiled. Outside was the fire escape he had hoped to find.

"Bingo!" he said. "Our ticket out of here." Joe slid the window open and looked down. Far below, men were scrambling over the lawn. "Maybe not. They're already waiting for us down there."

Frank grabbed a handful of files as the pounding on the door grew louder. He walked to the window and looked up. The fire escape continued up and curved onto the roof. Keys were now jingling outside the door.

"We've got no choice," Frank said. "We go up." They climbed onto the fire escape, which wobbled under their weight. But it seemed as if no one below saw them as they scaled the ladder to the roof. The roof was flat, with several pipes sticking out of it, and a large shedlike structure in one corner. In the structure was a door.

Stairs from inside, Frank realized. So they'll be coming at us from two directions. If only we could wreck the fire escape, he thought. But that would take tools they didn't have.

"Bad move, brother." Joe stood at the far edge of the roof, looking down and holding the AK47. "It's too long a drop to the ground—" He stared glumly at the nearest building, twenty feet away. "And the next roof's too far to jump to."

Anxiously, Frank turned in a circle, studying the roof. There had to be some way to escape, he insisted to himself, but he knew he was wrong.

His shoulders slumped. "I hate to say it," he said finally. "But unless we grow wings in the next few seconds, we're trapped."

Chapter

7

JOE PEERED OVER at the roof next door, so near and yet so far. "Look at those pipes," he said. "If only we had a rope or cable, we could lasso a pipe on the roof next door and run a line across to it."

"We can!" Frank cried, excited. He dropped the files to the roof. "I need the rifle."

Puzzled, Joe threw the AK47 to his brother. Frank snatched it in midair as he ran to the fire escape. "What are you doing?" Joe asked.

"No time to explain," Frank answered. He pointed at the door to the stairs. "Whatever you do, keep that door closed!" Then Frank was gone, climbing down the fire escape as it bounced beneath his feet.

He slipped back into Vladimir's office. Outside, keys clanged as the doorknob rattled. They're trying to find the right key, Frank realized. Vladimir must not be in the building any longer. Frank opened the fire closet in Vladimir's wall and pulled out the fire hose.

He turned the metal ring attaching the hose to the wall until the hose came free. The tough canvas hose would make as good a line as any.

As Frank gathered up the hose, he heard a key finally turning in the lock. He had to keep the guards from coming through the door.

His glance fell on the heavy bookcases with their thick books stacked around the doorway. With a grin he pulled the trigger on the AK47, spraying the top shelves. The books absorbed the bullets.

But the guards outside didn't know that. Frank could hear frantic commands as the men threw themselves to the floor.

Frank snatched the ax, and with a swift flick of his wrist he spun the wheel in the fire closet. A jet of water rushed from the wall where the hose had been and sprayed across the office. That ought to slow them down, he thought as he dashed to the window.

He was wrong. Like trained combat troops, the Russians rolled into the room and took positions on the floor. As Frank stepped onto the fire escape, they locked their sights on him and fired.

Vladimir's window fell into place behind Frank, and the shots bounced harmlessly off the bulletproof glass. Seconds later Frank climbed onto the roof.

"Great!" said Joe when he saw the fire hose. Frank handed him the ax instead.

"They're right behind me," Frank said. "But that fire escape's about to go. I don't think anyone's checked it in years. Try to pry it loose from the building with the ax."

"I do not understand," Elena said as Joe worked at the bolts holding the fire escape to the building. "How do we escape?"

"We're going to go hand over hand across this hose to the next building," replied Joe.

"I can't do it, my arms are too weak," Elena said.

"You'll hang onto me, and I'll take us both across. But right now I need some help. . . ."

Frank knotted one end of the hose around a pipe and tested it. The hose held. He tied the other end of the hose in a slipknot.

Joe groaned. "It's too late." The first Russian was slipping out of the window onto the fire escape. He grinned viciously up at Joe. The Russian's foot slammed down on the first rung of the ladder.

Under his weight the fire escape gave way. Flailing amid the falling metal, the Russian grabbed the window ledge and stopped his fall, but the fire escape crashed down to the ground.

"False alarm," Joe said. "How's it going on your end, Frank?"

"I think I've got the range," Frank said. He swung the looped end of the hose over his head like a lariat, then let go and flung it across to the other roof.

It bounced off a pipe, slipped off the building, and fell.

"Here," said Joe, taking the hose from Frank. "Let me show you how it's done."

"Hurry!" Elena screamed. Footsteps were pounding up the inside stairs.

We only need another minute, thought Frank. He studied the door to the stairwell. It had no lock. Metal braces stuck out of either side of the doorframe, but they were useless without a bar to hold the door closed.

A bar! he realized. He snatched up the ax and ran to the door. "Get back!" he ordered Elena, and she moved to the side. The door swung open, and Frank kicked out, driving a man back into the stairwell. Elena threw her weight into the door and slammed it shut, and Frank rammed the ax handle into place across the two braces.

"That won't hold them long," he told Joe. "Any luck?"

Joe focused on a curved pipe on the far roof.

He threw the hose across the alley. It caught the pipe. He pulled it taut.

"Let's go," he said. Frank scooped up the files as Elena rushed to Joe's side.

"Grab onto me," Joe said to Elena. "And hold tight." He lowered himself and Elena onto the hose and started to inch across the rope.

After only a foot of very slow going they heard the sound of wood splintering. The ax handle was breaking.

"You'll never make it all the way across," Frank whispered. "You'll get gunned down."

"We have to try," said Joe.

"Maybe not," Frank answered. And he signaled them to hurry back.

As Joe worked his way back the short distance, Frank said, "Here's my plan. . . ."

With a crack the ax handle split and shattered, the door swung open, and Russians swarmed onto the rooftop. They stopped, staring at one another in confusion.

Aside from the Russians, the rooftop was deserted.

Konstantin strolled onto the roof, and the Russians snapped to attention. He walked to the hose, still stretched to the far building, and looked over the edge of the roof. On the ground, halfway across the alley, were files and the AK47. On the far roof were more scattered files.

"How could you let them escape?" roared an angry voice behind him. Konstantin turned to see Vladimir standing in the doorway.

He waved Vladimir to the roof's edge. "They have reached the next house. Your men should search the streets. On foot they cannot get far." Almost as an afterthought he added, "They seem to have some of your files."

"What are you waiting for?" Vladimir told his men. "Bring them back."

The Russians raced down the stairs. Vladimir followed them slowly. On the roof Konstantin gazed at the nearby houses in the peaceful Spanish morning. Below, a wave of Russians broke through the streets. "Clever boys," Konstantin said, chuckling, then abruptly turned and went downstairs.

"All gone," Frank said. He rolled off the top of the structure that housed the stairwell, landed on the roof, and stretched his legs.

"I was so afraid," Elena said as Joe helped her down. "Lying so still, trying not to make a sound—"

Joe dropped to the roof. "You did fine. That was a good idea, Frank, throwing the files and rifle off the roof to make them think we'd made it to the other side."

"There was almost nothing in the files we could use," Frank said. "And the rifle wouldn't have done us much good against all those men. We didn't have anything to lose. This place should have cleared out by now. How can we get away from here?''

''I have a car parked just a block away,'' Elena said.

''Sounds like our best shot,'' Frank agreed. Going downstairs, they moved cautiously through the almost deserted consulate.

Elena turned onto a narrow dirt road. A short distance farther she pulled the Audi to a stop. ''Well, where do we go?'' she asked.

''Let's get out of the car for a minute and then discuss it,'' Joe answered her.

''We have to find the Network—if we can,'' Frank said. ''They're at the bottom of this whole mess.''

''You're right,'' said a deep voice. ''But the Network found you instead.'' Both Frank and Joe recognized the man who appeared just behind them. Usually he wore a gray suit and a rumpled trench coat. That day he was in short sleeves, with a camera around his neck—a typical tourist. His specialty was appearing completely unremarkable, just one more face in the crowd. But he really was a dangerous agent.

''The Gray Man!'' Joe said. Whenever they dealt with the Network, they had always worked through him. "Are we glad to see you! You've got to help us clear our names."

"I can't, Joe." He drew his hand from his slightly baggy pants. He held a small pistol. "I have my orders," the Gray Man said. "You're coming with me."

Chapter

8

"YOU'RE KIDDING!" JOE said. But the Gray Man's expression told him it was no joke. "Take us in for what?"

"Washington thinks you killed our agent here," the Gray Man explained. He waved the gun to signal them to raise their hands. "I'm to bring you in before the Spanish grab you. We don't want this to become more of an incident than it already is."

Frank slowly edged left. "Do you think we did it?"

The Gray Man shrugged. "What I think doesn't matter. To the Network you're outsiders. And that makes you suspect. The theory is you got greedy, stole the data Martin gave you, and decided to go into business for yourself. He tried to stop you and you killed him."

"Business?" Frank said. As the Gray Man's eyes followed Frank, Joe eased to the right. "Like *selling* the data? We don't even know what it is. How are we supposed to sell it?"

"You're not stupid, Frank, so don't play dumb with me," the Gray Man said. "In his last message, Martin said he passed the data on to you. If he said he did, he did."

Frank pondered the Gray Man's words. Had Martin passed the information to them without their knowing it? Was it in something he said? Or something he gave them? He reached for his pocket, and the Gray Man took aim at him.

"Slowly," the Gray Man said. "Two fingers."

Frank nodded, and dug into his back pocket with his thumb and index finger. Their itinerary was still there. He pulled it out. "This is the only thing Martin gave us," he said. "If this isn't it, I don't know what it is."

"Give it to the girl," the Gray Man ordered. Frank handed the paper to Elena. "Bring it here." She walked to the Gray Man, who took the paper in his free hand. As Elena returned to Frank, the Gray Man shook the paper open and studied it.

"This was printed from a computer," the Gray Man said. He crumpled the paper and threw it to the ground. "That wasn't Martin's style. To keep up his cover as a writer, he used a battered old manual typewriter. The *E* and the *J* were crooked. He didn't write this. Stop playing games.''

"The chauffeur said Martin gave it to him to give to us," Joe insisted, taking another step to the right.

"Chauffeur? The Network didn't arrange for a chauffeur."

Frank's jaw dropped. "Arrange? It was part of the contest I won."

"You won because you were the only entry," said the Gray Man. "It wasn't my idea. The Network needed a go-between for this exchange, someone who wasn't publicly connected to us.

"One of our people suggested you. When I told them you wouldn't go along with it, they created the phony contest. Once you were in Málaga, Martin would handle you."

He sighed. "I objected to the plan, but I was outvoted."

"Because your agent *had* to be rescued," Frank said. "I can understand that, but the Network still had no right to involve us."

"Who told you about our agent?" The Gray Man asked, suspicion creeping into his voice. "I thought you didn't talk to Martin about it."

"As a matter of fact, it was a guy named Konstantin," Frank said, inching left.

It was the Gray Man's turn to be surprised, and

for a moment it showed on his face. "Konstantin's here?" he said.

Joe nodded. "Do us a favor," he said. "*Talk* to us. Pretend for a minute that we walked into the middle of this, and tell us what's going on. Maybe if we know what this information is, we can tell you where to find it."

"I owe you that much," the Gray Man replied. "Martin had discovered the name of a mole—a double agent—inside the KGB. He was working for the Chinese too. That's why they were willing to let our man go.

"Stop it," he said suddenly.

Joe and Frank froze. They were standing directly opposite each other, with the Gray Man in the middle. The Gray Man knew that they had been trying to outflank him all along. "We're not going back with you," Joe said. "The only way to take us is to shoot us."

The Gray Man shook his head. "Don't be stupid."

"We've been set up," Joe said. "And our only hope is to prove that."

"I want to believe you. But I've already spent too much time talking about this." His face hardened. "Now, take out your pistol and throw it down the hill, Frank. Yes, I can see you've got one."

With two fingers Frank pulled the pistol from

his pants pocket and cast it away. "We don't want to hurt you," he said.

"That's nice," the Gray Man said. "I'd hate shooting you too."

Joe took a deep breath and charged. Maybe the Gray Man's reluctance would slow down his trigger finger. . . . He leapt in, feinting with his left. As the Gray Man slapped Joe's left arm aside, Joe drove a powerhouse right at the Gray Man's stomach.

But before the punch could land, the Gray Man swerved. His elbow hooked down around Joe's wrist, and the Gray Man's hand wrapped around Joe's shoulder. He spun on his heel and jerked forward. With a loud slap Joe slammed facedown into the dirt. The Gray Man had decked him without even using his gun.

Elena screamed and scampered off.

Frank circled slowly around the Gray Man. Their eyes locked and focused. He's going to beat me, Frank thought as he stared at the look of confidence on the man's face. No, he told himself. He's psyching me out. I'm going to win. I *have* to win. With a sharp cry Frank hurled himself forward, kicking out at the Gray Man's gun hand.

Once again the Gray Man didn't use his gun. His free hand shot out and cracked into Frank's chest, knocking him backward. Frank landed on his back with a thud.

"Finished?" the Gray Man asked. Angrily, Frank and Joe got to their feet. "Let me put it another way. You *are* finished." The gun was pointing dead at them. "Prove your innocence when you get home."

"No!" Elena shouted. She stood a few feet away. In her hand was the gun Frank had thrown away. "Get your hands up," she told the Gray Man. "Now!"

The Gray Man dropped his gun and cupped his hands together in back of his head. Joe scooped up the gun, and Frank yanked the camera from around the Gray Man's neck. With Elena keeping the gun aimed, the Hardys led the agent to a tree.

"Sorry we have to do this," Frank said. He pulled the Gray Man's arms back around the tree and tied them with the camera strap.

"We'll have a chance to talk again," the Gray Man called after them as they ran back to their car. "Real soon."

Moments later the car screeched back onto the main road, passing a gray sedan parked at the junction. "The Gray Man's," Frank said. "He's a very slick tail. I was looking, and never knew we were being followed."

"Think he'll be all right up there?" Joe asked. "Maybe we shouldn't have left him tied up."

"Him? He's probably free already," Frank said, rolling his window down. "You know, we're running out of time. We really have to figure this thing out.''

"I've been thinking about this mole in the KGB," Joe said, glancing out at the rocky hillside as they rushed past. "Suppose he found out about the exchange? If I were in that guy's shoes, I'd want to stop it."

Taking one hand off the steering wheel, Frank snapped his fingers. "Sure, that makes sense. He could learn a lot by putting himself close to Martin—maybe in disguise."

"Exactly, he could disguise himself as a chauffeur," Joe said. "Yeah, why else would that chauffeur pass a note to us and claim it was from Martin—for that matter, what other reason would he have for going around wearing a false beard and nose? He killed Martin, and *he* probably got the information everybody seems to think we got."

"Maybe not," Frank said. "This guy didn't take off. He hung around after Martin was dead. Remember the next day? Why would he do that if he had the data? I'm betting our mole doesn't have it yet."

Joe thought about it. "So we can still catch him."

"Right." To Elena in the back seat Frank said, "We're going to head back to our hotel. We'd better split up at that point. You're in this thing too deep as it is."

"Too deep to leave," Elena told him. "The Russians think I betrayed them. If they find me now, they'll—" She shuddered. "No, I'm safer staying with you two."

"We won't let anything happen to you." Joe glanced in the rearview mirror. A small red car was speeding along on the empty stretch of road behind them. "Frank? I think we might have company," he warned.

After looking in the mirror, Frank frowned. "Yeah, I noticed that car before, right after we left the Soviet consulate. Could be nothing, but then again—"

The red car sped up, zipping suddenly to the left to pass them. Frank glanced at it suspiciously, reaching for one of the pistols.

But a woman he'd never seen before was driving the red compact. Her eyes were hidden by sunglasses, and long dark hair swirled over her face and fell to meet a high collar that covered her neck.

She smiled warmly at Frank, and she raised a cigarette holder with a long cigarette in it to her lips.

Frank relaxed. "Nothing to worry about," he decided.

A thick swirl of smoke spat from the tip of the cigarette and shot across the space between the two cars. The smoke hit Frank in the face.

He coughed, suddenly let go of the wheel, and clutched at his throat with both hands.

The red car was already past them, speeding away.

For an instant Joe stared at his choking brother. "Frank, what's wrong?"

Frank tried to catch his breath but couldn't. "Smoke," he gasped. "Poison—" He fell against the steering wheel of the speeding car. "Woman—KGB—poisoned me—"

From the backseat Elena pointed and screamed.

Joe glanced up through the front windshield and grabbed for the steering wheel.

The road ahead took a sharp curve around a cliff. Far below the road was a stretch of bright blue sea. If Joe didn't get control, they'd be off the road and in the air.

Desperately, Joe tried to steer the careening Audi.

The car swerved wildly across the road. Its motion threw the unconscious Frank against his brother.

Joe lost his grip on the wheel.

Right in front of them now was a low wooden rail. The car was rushing straight at it.

The rail was all that stood between them and the long drop to the rocky beach.

Chapter

9

Joe shoved against his brother's unconscious body and got one hand on the steering wheel.

He gave it a sharp twist and with his other hand yanked at the emergency brake.

The Audi rattled, shuddered, and scraped against the wooden railing. Then it groaned and jerked to a stop, just inches from the edge.

Joe jumped out and glanced down the road as he hurried around the front of the car. "There's a truck blocking the road down there—holding up that red car. We can still catch her."

He ran to the driver's side, opened the door, and tugged Frank out from behind the wheel.

"I'm going to put him in the back, Elena. You drive," he told her.

A moment later they were off.

The road ahead was clear again, and the red car was growing ever smaller in the distance.

Elena slammed the gas pedal to the floor. "We should take him to the hospital," she suggested. "He may be dying."

"I'm sure he is," Joe said in a low voice. "But if he was right about that woman being a KGB assassin, a hospital won't help him. By the time they find what poisoned him, he'll be dead. No, our only hope is to catch up to the assassin."

They were reaching more heavily traveled roads now. The red car moved slower, but even so, the distance between it and the Audi kept growing.

"She is losing us," Elena cried. "How can she help your brother?"

"When KGB assassins use poison, they always carry an antidote, in case they should accidentally poison themselves," Joe replied grimly. "She's got it, and it's the only thing that will save Frank."

The street widened into a boulevard, with a grassy strip between the two sides of the road. The red car was still in view, far ahead. "You *are* a spy!" Elena said to Joe. "How else could you know so much about the KGB?"

Joe chuckled in spite of himself. "We're not spies, Elena, just ordinary Americans. There are plenty of books published about the KGB and how they operate. I've read one or two of them."

70

His smile faded as the red car vanished from sight, and he looked at his brother.

Frank was still breathing, but in a shallow, uneven way. His skin was tinged with blue. "He's suffocating." Joe's fists clenched as he looked for the red car. But it was gone. "We've failed."

"Not yet!" Elena said, determined. She spun the steering wheel left and hit the gas again. The Audi bounced on the low curb and sped onto the boulevard's center strip. The Hardy's car skidded wildly on the grass, its tail swaying back and forth, but Elena gripped the wheel and kept control.

They sped along the center strip, passing the traffic clogging the road, tearing through shrubs and flower beds. The red car came back into view—still far ahead. Joe bent forward in his seat. "Go," he urged Elena, and she sped even faster. Frank's life was in Elena's hands.

"Look out!" Joe shouted suddenly. Elena took her eyes off the red car and saw a clump of trees dead ahead, covering the width of the center strip. There was no way through it, and no time to stop. Elena slammed her foot on the brake and froze. Barely slowing, the car hurtled on toward the trees.

Joe reached over, spinning the steering wheel. The car swerved left, ran off the median, and sped headlong into the oncoming traffic. Cars ran off the road to avoid the Audi, and horns blared as it zipped past them. Elena stared straight ahead, her hands still gripping the wheel.

"Snap out of it!" Joe barked. "Frank needs you." At the sound of his voice Elena shook as if waking from a dream. With a gasp she slammed the brake and turned the wheel, and, tires screaming, the Audi pulled back onto the median, on the other side of the trees.

"The red car," she said, pointing to a compact on the right side of the median. Joe saw the dark-haired woman in it and smiled without humor.

"She's slowed down," he said. "She must think she lost us. Is she in for a surprise!"

The Audi jumped off the median and swung into traffic, sideswiping the red car. The woman looked up, startled, her face still obscured by sunglasses and wisps of black hair. But her lips tightened in anger as she saw Joe's face, and she aimed the cigarette holder toward him.

"Hit her again," Joe ordered, and Elena rammed the Audi into the red car a second time. The cigarette holder tumbled from the woman's fingers in the impact. It hung in midair for a second as she desperately grabbed for it. She missed. The holder fell out the car window and shattered on the ground, spewing glass pellets which broke and gave off wisps of poisoned smoke. In trying to catch the holder, the woman let go of her steering wheel.

The little red car screamed across the lanes and

smashed into a storefront, scattering fruit and vegetables all over the street. As the Audi pulled to a stop behind it, Joe looked at Elena admiringly. "Where'd you learn to drive like that?" he asked.

"American television," she replied. Then her eyes widened as the woman scrambled from the red car. "She's getting away!" Elena shouted.

"Not if I can help it," Joe replied. "Stay here with Frank." He leapt from the Audi and ran after the woman, who sprinted down the line of stores.

Joe closed in. The woman turned into the nearest alley and vanished from sight for a moment, but Joe wasn't worried. He knew she couldn't outrun him. He rounded the corner—and stopped.

The woman was gone.

It's not possible, he thought. The alley ended at a brick wall, and there was no way over it. Cautiously, Joe tried the doors on the alley. None opened. The woman couldn't have escaped.

Finally, he tried a pair of old wooden doors set into the ground. They swung up to reveal wooden steps and a dark basement below. He listened. From deep in the darkness came a muffled panting.

The woman was there.

He slowly moved down into the pitch-black of

the basement. There was no sound now. Two steps, and no sign of the woman. Three steps.

Strong hands grabbed his ankle, tugged, and Joe pitched down the last stairs. He rolled, landing faceup, and in the dim light he caught the faint gleam of a small revolver aimed at him.

"You will not live to blackmail me," came a gritted whisper from the dark. "You, your brother, Martin—you should never have played games with me." A finger tightened on the trigger.

Joe kicked fiercely and knocked the gun into the air as the shot rang out. He did a backward flip and landed on his feet as the woman started up the steps. Without thinking, Joe lunged at her, grabbing at her purse and her hair. Both tore loose in his grip, and he fell back down the stairs, landing on the basement floor with a thud. The woman vanished into the alley.

Seconds later Joe emerged into the light. He started back to the Audi.

"Quick," Elena said as she saw him. She held Frank, whose breathing had all but stopped. "You got the antidote from the woman?"

Joe opened the purse, rifled through it, and brought out a small clear bottle with Russian lettering on it. "This had better be it," he said, and handed it to Elena, who opened it and forced the contents through Frank's lips.

Frank sputtered and convulsed as the liquid

flowed into his mouth. With a great spasm he went limp in Elena's arms.

"He's not breathing," Elena said, terrified. "I think he's dead!"

"Am—not," Frank mumbled, and opened his eyes. "What happened?"

"Oh, nothing," Joe said, relieved. "You just got poisoned by a KGB agent."

"Joe caught her," Elena said excitedly.

Joe flushed and shook his head. "No, I didn't," he admitted. "And it wasn't a her."

"What?" Frank and Elena said at the same time.

Joe held up the wig. "A disguise. When she spoke, she had a man's voice—also disguised—and she wore men's shoes. I got a pretty good look at them. It was a man disguised as a woman."

"The chauffeur was a disguise too," Frank said. He sat up weakly in the car. "Probably the same person. And that assassination attempt means he's probably a member of Department V."

"Or was," Joe said. "It could have been Vladimir."

"We must go somewhere so you can rest," Elena told Frank. "Your hotel?"

Frank shook his head weakly. "The police might be waiting for us there. Any way we can get out of town without running into cops?"

"Certainly," Elena said. "We can follow the dirt roads along the hills and go south along the Costa del Sol. There is a resort village called Marbella not too far away."

"Anywhere we won't get chased or shot at is okay with me," Joe replied. Elena started the car, and they wound through the foothills of the Sierra Nevada Mountains. They could see the highway that hugged the coastline but were far removed from it. The hillsides were dotted with small pastel-colored houses.

"I cannot believe Vladimir is an assassin," Elena said after some time.

"So why'd you save us from him at the consulate?" Joe asked.

"It was that man, Konstantin," Elena said. "Electricity." She swallowed in disgust. "He would have killed you."

"I don't think so," Frank replied. He thumbed through the one file he had taken from Vladimir's office. "Konstantin just wanted to scare us."

"That doesn't make him a nice guy though," Joe said.

Frank pulled a map of the Spanish coast out of the file. On it, the town of Torremolinos was circled in red. He held up the map so Elena could see it. "Does this mean anything?"

"Vladimir's villa is there," Elena replied, glancing at the map. "I went there once."

"Hmmm," Frank said, setting down the map

76

and picking up another piece of paper. "Here's a memo from some KGB agent accusing Vladimir of anti-Soviet activities. He probably intercepted before it got to his superiors."

"Maybe they did get the message. That could be why he's stuck in Spain," Joe said, chuckling.

Then he stopped laughing, his eyes opening wide. Joe looked at Frank. He had the same expression on his face.

"Vladimir's the mole!" they said at the same time.

Frank settled back in his seat. "That would explain why the KGB sent Konstantin in to look after things. They suspect Vladimir." He made a fist and chewed on his knuckle as he thought. "Elena, who brought you in to contact us?"

"Vladimir," Elena said.

"And who were you supposed to give the information to?"

"Vladimir," Elena replied.

"Where was he the morning of the contact?" Frank continued.

"I don't know," she said uncertainly.

"Yeah, he could have been the chauffeur," Joe said. "What's that noise?"

Frank heard it too, a soft whirring growing louder each second. He stared out the window at the sky.

"Helicopter!" Frank shouted over the noise. "No markings. It's not the police."

77

Something flashed from the side of the helicopter and screamed toward them.

The ground erupted in smoke and thunder, throwing Frank out the window as the car swayed on two wheels. It crashed back to the ground as the helicopter fired another missile.

An explosion in front of the Audi brought it to a halt and spattered it with dirt. The car half vanished in the gathering smoke.

As Frank watched helplessly from the roadside, a third missile screamed down. Shock waves hurled him back as the car went up in a ball of fire.

"Joe!" Frank called as he picked himself up off the ground. "Joe!"

No sound came from the Audi except a steady crackling, and no movement but the dancing of the flames.

Chapter
10

"JOE!" FRANK CRIED out again. He tried to reach the burning car, but the heat and smoke forced him back.

I've got to keep yelling so Joe and Elena can find their way out of the flames, Frank told himself. Joe has survived worse than this. I can't give up. I can't. But even as he shouted, Frank wondered how long he could keep convincing himself.

The beating of the rotors drowned out his voice as the helicopter landed on the road a few yards from the wreck. The pilot got out, holding a rifle. Out from the other side stepped an agent Frank recognized. The agent flashed Frank an unpleasant smile, and Frank could feel his grief burn away into anger.

"Your foolishness cost your brother his life,"

the pilot said. "Do not resist, or the same will happen to you." He cradled the rifle in the crook of his arm, leveling it at Frank.

Frank clenched his fists. Just stay cool, he told himself. They had killed Joe, and they had to pay for it. Hot anger wasn't going to help him. He had to cool down. He had to stay alive and make them pay.

The Russians walked toward him, and Frank backed away from them. "Stop," ordered the pilot, his finger pulling back on the trigger.

"Go ahead," Frank said, surprised by the coldness in his own voice. "Shoot. You'd like that. Vladimir would like that. Then he'd never get the information he wants, would he? It'd be out there, waiting for someone else to find it. I can just imagine what he'd do to the men who kept him from getting it."

The smile faded from the agent's lips. He shot a worried glance at the pilot, who seemed unconcerned. Frank turned away from them and began walking, but as he took his fifth step, the pilot fired. The shot sprayed up a jet of dirt just inches in front of Frank's feet. He stopped.

"But Konstantin will not mind," the pilot said, laughing. "Hands up, please." Frank raised his hands. "Come here."

Frank marched toward them. His bluff had failed, he realized, and if he tried to run from the rifle, it would cut him down. He stared bitterly at the burning car as he headed back.

All of a sudden Frank stopped, startled. "Come," the pilot repeated, and Frank began walking again, his face toward the ground to keep them from realizing what he had seen.

In the smoke something had moved, then vanished behind the helicopter.

With the rifle the pilot nudged Frank toward the helicopter. He circled in front of Frank to lead the way, backing up to keep Frank covered. The silent agent followed on Frank's heels, ready to block any escape attempt. At last the pilot backed through the helicopter door, signaling Frank to follow.

But something moved behind the pilot, inside the helicopter. Joe! His face was streaked with smoke, and he looked grim as he slammed into the pilot's back, knocking him out of the helicopter. Frank grabbed the rifle with both hands, rolled into a backward somersault, and, kicking upward, threw the surprised pilot over his head and into the silent agent.

They tumbled to the ground, and then Frank and Joe were on them. When Frank and Joe stood, the pilot and the agent were unconscious.

"Am I glad to see you!" Frank said, giving his brother a hug. "How?"

"Luck, mostly," Joe replied. "When you got knocked out of the car, I guessed what was coming next, so I grabbed Elena and pulled her out the other side." He whistled. From behind a bush Elena appeared. "I'm not sure what happened next. An explosion, I guess, and when I woke up, I saw those jerks hauling you off. So I snuck around to the other side of the chopper and got in to surprise them."

"You saved my life," Elena said.

"No problem," Joe said, a bit embarrassed. He looked at the remains of the Audi. The fire was almost out, leaving a blackened husk. "It's a cinch we're not going anywhere in that. Maybe we ought to turn back."

"No," Elena said. "Marbella is only five kilometers more. Perhaps less."

"About three miles, then," Frank said. "We'd better get walking." Joe and Elena stared at him. "It's safer and less conspicuous than hitchhiking," he explained. "And none of us knows how to fly a chopper, right?"

"When you're right, you're right." Joe picked up the rifle in both hands, twirled it over his head, and let it go. It disappeared into a tree. "No sense leaving it for the Russians. Should we tie them up with their belts?"

Frank nodded.

As soon as they were finished, they began the long hike to Marbella.

*   *   *

"I hope this works," Joe said the next day. He was basking in the morning sun, refreshed after a good night's sleep in a soft bed. It now seemed like the day before had never happened. But he did remember everything. They had reached Marbella, checked into a hotel, and made plans over dinner.

"I don't see why it won't," Frank answered. They stood on a crest overlooking the harbor of Marbella, which was filled with yachts. "Elena kept up her end. A family's willing to take us back to Málaga on their private boat, so that'll get us past all the roadblocks."

"Think the desk clerk bought our stories?" Joe asked.

"After I asked him all those questions about how to get from Algeciras to Morocco?" Frank said. "Sure. He'll be able to identify us to the police all right."

"But will they buy it?" Joe wondered out loud.

"After we phone in a tip to Inspector Melendez, they ought to. While they're trying to keep us from getting to Africa, we can search our hotel room and Martin's in Málaga."

They walked past a row of boutiques and restaurants. Stopping in front of a swimwear shop, Joe studied the window. "You know," he said, "the boat ride to Málaga will last awhile. If I bought a suit, I could work on my tan on the way. And I did come to Spain to work on my tan."

"Dream on, brother," Frank said. He glanced at his watch. "Elena said we have to be on that yacht at nine A.M. sharp, or we'll get left behind." He stiffened. "Joe, look straight ahead, and whatever you do, don't turn around."

Puzzled, Joe stared in the window and gasped. On the other side of the street, reflected in the shop window, was a policeman. "He couldn't be looking for us, could he?" he whispered to Frank.

"I don't know," Frank whispered back. "Start walking. Slowly."

They sauntered down the street, leaving the policeman behind. As they turned a corner, they saw another policeman ahead of them, and, a block farther along, another.

The Hardys ducked into a doorway and waited for a third to pass.

"The harbor's crawling with cops," Joe realized when the policeman had walked by. "They *must* be after us."

"It's not possible," Frank said as they returned to the street. He looked at his watch again. It read 8:55. "Not unless— What if Elena sold us out?"

"Couldn't be," Joe replied. "Not after all we've been through together. More likely the hotel clerk got itchy and called the cops."

"We'll find out when we reach the harbor," Frank decided. "Or sooner." Another policeman walked straight toward them. There was no time to duck out of sight, and turning around would attract his attention. They would have to brazen it out.

He looked them up and down as they passed, but did nothing. Joe breathed easier. It had been simple, almost too simple, and he looked over his shoulder to get another look at the policeman's reaction.

He saw the policeman raise a whistle to his lips.

"Run," Joe yelled as a shrill whistle pierced the air. The Hardys sprinted off with the policeman close behind. Ahead lay the harbor, and the Hardys could see swarms of boats, all shapes and sizes, as they neared. But there was no sign of Elena.

Other policemen joined in the chase. "We're in luck," Frank said as he ran. "If you can call this luck. I don't think they've sealed off the harbor yet. That means all the cops are behind us."

They reached the harbor and dashed from pier to pier, looking for the boat. Where's Elena, Joe wondered. Maybe she did set us up.

No, he thought, and put the idea out of his mind. But they couldn't find Elena or the boat. More whistles sounded from all directions. The police were closing in.

"Look!" Frank shouted. "There she is!"

Elena stood in the stern of a large boat with

sails of aqua and gold. She was staring sadly at them.

Between them and the boat were fifty feet of water.

Trapped at the end of a pier, the Hardys watched the sailboat drift away, moving out to sea.

Chapter

11

THE HARDYS SLOWLY turned around. A semicircle of policemen had formed at the other end of the pier. They linked hands, barring any path of escape, and walked slowly toward the Hardys.

"Great," Joe said. "What do we do now?"

"The way I see it," Frank replied, "we fight or we surrender."

"What's the worst that could happen if we surrender?" Joe asked, though the grim humor in his voice told Frank he wasn't really serious. "We get thrown in a Spanish jail for what? Twenty, thirty years? Life maybe?" He clenched his fists and stood shoulder to shoulder with his brother, ready to do battle with the cordon of policemen.

Frank studied the crowd that was gathering to

watch on the dock. "If we fight, we could probably break through. But the police might start
shooting. Someone could get hurt."

"Us, more than likely," Joe growled. The policemen were ten feet away, and closing in. "I
guess there's only one thing to do."

Frank nodded. "One—two—three . . ."

At the count of three the Hardys took two steps
back and dropped from the pier into the ocean.
The policemen broke ranks and dashed to the end
of the pier. There was no sign of the Hardys, only
ripples on the water. Two policemen dived into
the water, stayed under for a few seconds, then
bobbed to the surface, shaking their heads. Others ran back down the pier and scattered the
length of the harbor, their eyes on the water.
They, too, had nothing to report. The Hardys
were gone.

Air trapped in his puffing cheeks, Joe swam
underwater, moving steadily away from the land.
The water above him looked golden with the
morning sun shining on it, but below was darkness. His lungs burned, and he desperately
needed to breathe.

He clamped his lips, holding the air in as he
passed under something long and dark. The hull
of a boat, he realized. Ahead he saw a soft glow,
and he knew that there, on the other side of the
boat, he could surface and breathe again, hidden
from the harbor.

Joe reached up, clawing toward the light. His chest ached. How long had he been under, he wondered, and he knew it was too long. His mouth burst open with a rush of air, and saltwater came flooding in. It stung his lips and tongue, and pushed down his throat, choking him. His water-logged clothes were dragging him down, but he kicked desperately, forcing himself up toward the light.

Sputtering and coughing, Joe broke through the surface of the sea, arching his back so that his face remained above water. As he floated and gulped the warm Mediterranean air, the sea churned in a bubbly froth, and a small wave splashed over him. From the middle of the wave burst Frank, gasping for life. Joe grabbed his brother's arm and held him up until Frank caught his breath too.

"Any sign of the cops?" Frank asked, still choking on the sea. They bobbed in the shadow of a moored yacht, hidden from the shore by it. Joe peered around the yacht's bow and studied the harbor.

"No," he said. "But it won't be long before they send boats out to look for us." Joe turned toward the open sea and saw the sailboat they should have been on drifting away from them, its gold- and aqua-striped sail waving at them like a flag. "Think we can catch it?"

Frank dabbed a finger on his tongue and stuck

the finger in the air. "Not much wind," he replied. "What choice do we have?"

Kicking off from the side of the yacht, they propelled themselves toward the drifting sailboat. With powerful strokes the Hardys cut through the warm blue water, moving farther and farther out to sea.

"Think there're any sharks or octopuses out here, Frank?"

"Let's hope we won't find out," Frank said, his eyes on the sailboat. It was closer now, carelessly washing eastward on gentle winds and currents. He could see Elena on the stern, still staring back at the harbor. "Only a few more yards."

"Hey!" Joe yelled as loud as he could, and Elena stiffened and looked around. Again he yelled, "Over here!" He treaded water and waved frantically. Elena shielded her eyes from the sun with her hand and gazed out over the water. A second later she stepped out of sight.

"Did she see us?" Frank asked. But before Joe could answer, he answered himself. "I wonder. I'm not sure we can trust her, Joe."

"We can trust her," Joe said. "Look at how she's helped us so far." But doubt was creeping into his voice. The sails on the boat had shifted, and the boat picked up speed, cruising away from them. Had she seen them, he wondered. Had she told the captain to leave them adrift there? It was the only explanation he could think of.

"Look!" Frank said excitedly. "It's turning." The wind had caught the sails and was moving the sailboat rapidly back toward them. "I take it all back," he told Joe. "Elena's great."

Ropes were tossed down as the sailboat cruised past them, and the Hardys grabbed the ropes and tied them around their waists. One by one they were pulled onto the deck, and Joe smiled at Elena as he rose.

"You were lucky the little lady saw you, boys," said one of the men who had brought them aboard. He was tall and red-faced, and his voice had a familiar twang. "And here we thought she was fooling us when she said some fellow Americans needed a ride. You oughtn't to have been late though. Made her look like a liar."

"Sorry about that. We ran into a little trouble. You're Texan?" Joe asked, unable to believe his ears. "I'm Joe, and this is my brother, Frank."

Frank nodded and peeled off his wet shirt.

"Sam," the Texan replied. He pointed to a rugged-looking man at the wheel. "That's Jimmy Luke. You boys easterners, hey? Well, I guess not everyone can be born lucky. You better get out of those wet clothes. The sun'll dry them out by the time we hit Málaga, and there are some swim trunks in the hold you can wear in the meantime."

"Thanks," Frank said. "When do you expect we'll reach Málaga?" He and Joe walked toward the hold.

"A couple hours at the rate we're going," Sam replied. "You all just relax and enjoy yourselves, y'hear?"

"Thanks again," Joe said. "We really appreciate this."

Sam winked. "Think nothing of it. What are countrymen for, right?" As the boat straightened out its course, he called after the Hardys, "But the next time you go swimming, you ought to dress for it."

"Is there something wrong?" Elena asked Frank as they climbed onto the pier at Málaga. Frank had been frowning.

"I'd still like to know how the cops knew to expect us at the harbor," he said. "You never explained that."

"I *cannot* explain," Elena said desperately. "I had nothing to do with it. You must believe me."

"We do," Joe said, stepping between her and his brother. "Inspector Melendez probably notified every cop on the Costa del Sol to be on the lookout for us. All it would have taken was for one to spot us. For all we know, they think we're in Algeciras by now, just as we planned."

"Look, I'm sorry," Frank said to Elena. "But

this is a life-or-death situation. We can't afford to ignore all the possibilities.''

"I forgive you." But Elena's voice trembled as she spoke. She pressed close to Joe, and he put a comforting arm around her. "I only wanted to help."

"You have," Joe said, and he glowered at Frank. "A lot. If that's settled, we'd better figure out where we go from here."

"The bus," Frank said, and both Joe and Elena stared at him in surprise. "We're running out of money," he explained, "so we'd better get to the hotel and try to get our travelers' checks. It'll be risky, but if the police are convinced we're on our way to Africa, security might be lax."

"Plus," Joe said, "if Martin really gave us something, it's got to be in our stuff. I think the only way we're going to crack this thing open is to find the information. So where do we catch a bus?"

"Right this way," Elena said.

After a slow, crowded ride back into central Málaga, they arrived in front of their hotel.

"It's quiet," Joe said as he stepped off the bus. "Too quiet. It might be a trap."

"No," said Elena. "Siesta time. It's customary during lunch for the stores to close up. Everyone goes home to eat and sleep. The hotel should be just as quiet."

They reached the front door and Frank looked

in. In the lobby three people sat in armchairs, reading papers. Only one man stood behind the main desk. "We've got to get in without being seen," he said. Then, to Elena he said, "Can you distract them?"

"Yes," Elena said. She left them and walked around the hotel until they could see her framed in the rear exit. "Help!" she screamed. "*Socorro!* Help!"

The desk clerk ran to the hall, and Elena disappeared from the back door as he rounded the corner and moved toward the exit. The guests in the lobby turned their heads toward the screaming.

In a flash Joe dashed through the lobby and slipped behind the front desk, grabbing the key to their room. He joined Frank at the stairwell, and together they sprinted up to the third floor. No one else was in the hallway.

Carefully, they leaned around the corner and looked down the hall. "They've taken the guard off the door," Frank said. "Let's go." They slipped silently to their room. Joe put the key into the lock, quickly turned it, and swung open the door. They darted in, shutting the door behind them.

Frank let out a sigh as he opened the closet door. Then he froze.

None of their luggage was there.

He frantically went over the room, then turned

to his brother. "The police took everything," Frank said, dismayed. "We've hit a dead end."

"That's a good way of putting it," said a voice behind them. As the Hardys turned, the door slammed shut.

"Now," the Gray Man continued as he stood in the narrow entrance hall. "Where were we?"

Chapter

12

JOE HURLED HIMSELF at the Gray Man. In the cramped area Joe hoped the Network agent wouldn't have space to maneuver.

The Gray Man ducked under Joe's swing, stood up, and drove his arm against Joe's back. Joe slammed into the wall and bounced off. The Gray Man caught him behind the knees, and then Joe was flying across the room. He sprawled on his bed as the Gray Man, hands in his pockets, sat in a chair near the door.

The government man sighed. "Frank, sit on your brother while we have a little chat."

Frank leaned on a wall and put his hands in his own pockets, keeping his eyes on the Gray Man. "What's there to talk about? You've got to take us in, right?"

"Maybe," the Gray Man replied. "Maybe not."

"Does this mean you believe we didn't kill Martin?" Frank asked.

"I wrote up your profiles for the Network, remember? Cold-blooded murder's just not in your makeup. Even if you had a motive, which you don't."

"Yeah," Joe said, sitting up on the bed. "But you said your boss wouldn't be satisfied."

"I've been thinking about that," the Gray Man said. "I had a lot of time to think yesterday. You might remember. Someone left me tied up to a tree."

"Sorry about that," Frank said. "We had to. You understand."

The Gray Man shrugged. "I would have done the same. But let me explain something to you. It doesn't matter if you're innocent or not. A deal with the Russians got messed up. The Network won't take the rap for that; it would look bad for our side. If they can lay the blame on the go-betweens, well, it's what happens sometimes when you use freelancers."

"That's not fair," Joe protested. "We didn't ask to get in the middle."

"Welcome to the spy business," the Gray Man answered. "Face it. You're what we in the business call 'out in the cold,' unless you can pull a rabbit out of your hat."

97

"Or a killer and a name," Frank said. "We sort of figured that out already. Why are you telling us all this?"

"I feel responsible for you," the Gray Man admitted. "I got you involved with the Network in the first place. So I'm going to help."

"Won't that upset your people?" Joe asked.

"We won't tell them," the Gray Man said. "They won't suspect anything for another twenty-four hours. That's our time limit. What have you got so far?"

"A theory," Frank replied. "Our most likely suspect for the murder is the KGB mole."

"Who is—?"

Frank shook his head. "That's the problem. We can't know for sure until we get our hands on Martin's information. Do you have any idea what it looked like?"

"None," the Gray Man said. "No one in Washington does either. That was Martin's department. He was a strange guy, a real loner." He rubbed his chin, thinking. "What's your girlfriend's role in this anyway? Ever consider that she might be your suspect?"

"We considered it," Frank began.

"No, we didn't," Joe interrupted angrily.

"No offense, Joe," the Gray Man said, "but I'll take Frank's word over yours in this case. You're a sucker for a pretty face." Joe reddened with embarrassment. "Frank, go on."

"We dismissed it," Frank said. "She's as innocent as we are. We think it's Vladimir, the KGB agent. And we think Martin did slip us the information to prove it—without telling us. But the cops got all our stuff, so how are we going to find it?"

"That is a problem," the Gray Man agreed. "Unless you knew that it was probably in the local police storage warehouse and that the warehouse is half a mile from the harbor."

"How did you know that?" Joe asked.

"It's my business, remember?" the Gray Man said. "If I showed you where it was, you think you could sneak in and get your things?"

"You make it sound so easy," Joe said.

"You'll find a way," the Network agent replied. "You have to. The mole's probably as eager to get his hands on the information as you are. You'd better get to it first."

"You're right. Let's go," Frank said. "It's still siesta for a couple of hours. We may as well hit the place now. They won't be expecting it, and it makes more sense than waiting around here to be caught."

"Elena goes with us," Joe insisted. "I'm not abandoning her. Not while the Russians are after her too."

The Gray Man stood and chuckled. "See what I mean. A pretty face." He opened the door and peeked into the empty hall, then waved the Hardys toward him. "Sure, bring her. The more the merrier."

The police storage warehouse was a long windowless hut made of steel. It had a curved roof and was surrounded by a chain-link fence. "Electrified?" asked Frank as he studied the building from across the street. The Gray Man nodded and put a finger to his lips, signaling Frank to keep silent. In front of the gate to the warehouse an armed policeman stood, waiting at the checkpoint, and just inside the gate were parked a dozen empty police cars.

"How do we know how many cops are in there?" Joe whispered.

"We don't," the Gray Man whispered back, pointing his finger at the gate. "That's the only way in. And out."

"How are we supposed to get by *him?*" Frank asked, nodding toward the sentry.

"I'll handle that," the Gray Man said. He took Elena by the arm. "You just get ready to make your move."

The Hardys watched Elena and the Gray Man vanish down the street. For long minutes they waited.

A shrill squeal pierced the air, then turned into a growing mechanical rumble.

"What's that?" Joe asked, and then he saw it. The Gray Man's car was racing down the street, swerving wildly. The guard looked up, shocked, and unbuttoned his holster. Before the Hardys' eyes, the car skidded off the pavement and rammed to a stop against a telephone pole.

The car burst into flames, and from the fire came a pleading female voice, pitifully calling, *"Socorro! Socorro!"*

"Elena!" Joe gasped, and started out from his hiding place. This was a special nightmare for him. He'd lost one girlfriend in a burning car. But Frank grabbed his arm and held him back. "She's in trouble, Frank. If you don't let go, I'll—"

"No," Frank said. "Look." The guard ran to the burning car, and from the hut came two other policemen. They, too, went to the car, but all three were forced back by the flames. "I don't know how they're doing it, but it's just her voice. It's our diversion."

Joe's face brightened. "Come on," he said. While the policemen's backs were turned, the Hardys sneaked across the street and through the gate. They ran into the building, slamming the door behind them. Two offices were on either side of the doorway. From there the hut opened into a giant warehouse filled with file cabinets and rows of steel shelves.

"No time to figure out the filing system," Frank said. "Look for our suitcases. They can't store too much luggage in here."

"You think so, do you?" Joe asked as he

moved down one of the aisles. He stared at a rack filled with baggage. Then he smiled.

On the top shelf was his carry-on bag, and Frank's sat a shelf down. "Over here," he called.

Quickly they dragged the bags down and opened them. "It's all here," Frank said as he rifled through his things. "Nothing's been taken out, but nothing's been added to mine either. What about yours?"

"Nothing," Joe muttered. "I was so sure this would be it. We'd better get this stuff back in place so the cops won't suspect we've been here."

"Let's make a couple of changes," said Frank. He peeled back the upper lining of his suitcase and pulled a stack of traveler's checks from behind it. Then he picked up his tape player, strapped it to his belt, and stuffed a couple of tapes into his pockets. "If I'm going to be on the run, I'm going to enjoy myself," he explained.

A nearby voice shouted in Spanish. Frank and Joe looked up the barrel of a gun.

"What's he saying?" Frank asked as he stood and raised his hands.

"A rough translation?" Joe replied, his hands also in the air. "We're going to a jail for a long, long time."

Chapter

13

"DON'T SHOOT," FRANK told the policeman. His hands outstretched, he took a step toward the cop. Puzzled, the policeman fixed his aim on Frank and barked out an order. But Frank slowly moved closer.

"He wants you to stop, Frank," Joe said. "He doesn't understand English."

Frank jerked to a halt and raised his hands again, staring wide-eyed at the policeman. He looked innocent, but his words weren't. "That's all I need to know. When I tell you to, hit the floor. Fast."

"Don't make a move. He'll shoot." Joe translated the cop's words, his eyes on the gun aimed at his brother's chest. Without thinking, he moved toward Frank. Startled, the policeman pivoted, pointing the gun at Joe.

"Now!" Frank shouted. He clutched the shelf to his right and pulled. The shelf toppled over, burying the policeman in a flood of boxes and stolen merchandise. The loot literally swept the cop off his feet, the gun flying from his hand and sliding under another set of shelves without going off.

"That was lucky. One shot and this place would have been crawling with cops," Frank said, digging the policeman out from under the boxes. He checked the cop's pulse and held a finger beneath his nose to test his breathing. Both were strong and steady. "He'll be all right, except for this forced siesta."

"Great," Joe said. "Let's get out while we have the chance."

Cautiously, they crept toward the door. Frank opened the door a crack and looked out toward the checkpoint and the street. Though a thin trail of dark smoke still rose into the air, the fire in the car was out.

The two policemen who had rushed out to help were coming back in.

Frank and Joe looked at each other. They were trapped. Three cops blocked the only way out of the warehouse. And behind them was another guard, who sooner or later was going to wake up and start hollering.

"Things can't get worse," Joe whispered.

He was wrong.

"More trouble," Frank said, still looking outside. "Take a peek at who just showed up."

Joe glanced out. Then he closed the door. "Vladimir and Konstantin. What bad timing!"

"And it doesn't take a genius to guess what they want," Frank said. "The same thing we wanted—Martin's information. They must've come to the same conclusion we did."

"But we were wrong," Joe said. "It wasn't in our stuff."

"But they don't know that." Frank opened the door a sliver and looked out again. The guards were arguing with the Russians, barring the entrance while Vladimir kept pointing at some sort of document and thrusting it into their faces.

"Another chance to put your Spanish to the test, Joe. Can you make this out?"

Joe put his ear to the door and listened. "As near as I can make out, Vladimir has an order from Inspector Melendez giving them access to our stuff. The head guard wants them to wait until Melendez verifies the order."

The talking outside slowly turned to shouting. "Sounds like Vladimir doesn't care for that idea."

"His authorization order is probably a forgery." Frank grinned. "I bet Vladimir's getting pretty nervous by now. Until he gets and destroys the information, his freedom's hanging by a thread." Outside, the voices rose.

"Konstantin seems to be taking the whole thing in stride." Joe peeked out. "This argument may be our best chance to get out of here—if we make our move quick."

"If we can de-electrify the fence, we can climb over it. They don't even have to see us," Frank said. He gazed around for a switch but saw nothing. "The control must be outside, at the guard post. That lets that out. We'd never get to it without being spotted."

"Something's happening," said Joe. At the checkpoint one guard was picking up a phone and reaching for his revolver.

Shaking his head, Konstantin held out his attaché case. It flipped open, and a cloud of gas burst out to envelop the three guards. They staggered back, then fell to the ground. Vladimir and Konstantin were both holding pads over their noses and mouths.

"Konstantin," came a voice outside the gate. The single word was punctuated by the telltale click of a bullet being jacked into the chamber of an automatic. Vladimir and Konstantin stiffened. They turned slowly.

The Gray Man stood there with an automatic trained on them.

"This is very foolish, my friend," Konstantin

scolded. "After we worked so well together in Paris."

"True, we'll always have Paris," the Gray Man replied. "But don't think we're friends. We're business associates, and we have problems to work out like civilized men."

Vladimir angrily pointed at the Gray Man. "You had your chance to save your agent," he said. "You will not see him again."

"Take it easy," the Gray Man said. "We can still work things out to everyone's satisfaction. Let's not abandon the swap over a silly misunderstanding."

"Misunderstanding?" Vladimir repeated coldly. "I for one do not—"

Konstantin raised a hand to silence him.

"Always you are the soul of logic, and I agree completely," Konstantin told the Gray Man. "We must, however, have some sign of your good intentions. A hostage, perhaps."

"I see three at your feet," the Gray Man said.

"We need someone more *personally* involved," Konstantin replied without blinking. "One of the young men. Where are they?"

"Right here," Frank said, throwing open the door behind the two Russians. "No hostages."

Vladimir whipped around at the sound of Frank's voice. When he saw the Hardys, his lips formed a hard line. But other than that he showed only icy calm. "These two young fools have stolen the name. Turn them over to us."

"Not true," the Gray Man said. "They've told me they didn't steal it, and I believe them. Someone else killed Martin. Your mole."

"Lies. A Network smear tactic," Vladimir said flatly. "You can prove nothing."

"I think we can, right now," the Gray Man replied, and to the Hardys he said, "Over here." They moved in a wide arc around the Russians. To Vladimir the Gray Man said, "I think we can. Tell us what you found in your luggage, Frank."

"Whatever Martin had, it wasn't there," Frank mumbled.

Vladimir's voice cut like a knife. "Even now they lie. We must not let them leave."

"Silence!" Konstantin barked. "Anyone can see these are honorable men." He smiled at Frank, saying, "I bow to your honesty," and he made a deep, comic bow, his head going almost all the way to his knees.

"Frank!" the Gray Man warned. "Look out!"

It was too late. From the bow Konstantin swept up one guard's revolver, and as his hands touched the ground, he balanced on them and swung his body around, catching his ankles in Frank's and knocking Frank off his feet.

They rose a second later. But now Konstantin stood behind Frank. His right arm wrapped tightly around Frank's neck, the other hand held the revolver.

"Ah. Now I have my hostage," Konstantin told the Gray Man.

Frank grabbed the arm across his throat and chinned himself on it, bringing his heels up against Konstantin's shins as hard as he could. The tall Russian howled and loosened his grip. Frank dropped to the ground, and he and Joe sprinted across the street.

"Stop!" Vladimir warned. He tore the revolver from Konstantin's grip and fired it recklessly.

"Get out of here!" the Gray Man ordered. He pushed Elena at Joe and fired back at Vladimir. "I'll handle this."

"We can't leave you," Frank said.

"I'll find you again, don't worry," the Gray Man answered. "If we take off together, they'll catch us in no time. If I hold them off, they'll lose your trail. Go." He stepped behind a tree and fired another shot around it.

"He is right," Elena said, and she tugged on their arms, pulling them away. Reluctantly, they left the Gray Man behind.

Siesta had ended, and crowds of people were back on the streets. "I wish we hadn't had to leave the Gray Man," Frank said.

"Say, how'd he pull off that car-crash stunt

anyway? I was afraid you were in the car," Joe said.

"A receiver," Elena admitted. "Part of the surveillance equipment he carries with him. I spoke into the microphone. He jammed the steering wheel of the car so it would move in a straight line when it rolled."

"Let's swap stories later," Frank said. "We're sitting ducks out here on the street. But where can we go?"

"I have friends," Elena said wearily. "I did not want to involve them, but now . . ." She sighed. "It is too far to walk." She went to the curb and stuck her thumb out.

"Hitchhiking's dangerous," Joe said. Elena ignored him. Three cars cruised by her, but the fourth came to a stop. She ran to it and scrambled into the front seat. The back door swung open, and Joe began to climb in. He stopped as he saw Elena trembling in front.

"Get in," Konstantin said, seated behind the steering wheel, a triumphant smile on his lips.

Chapter

14

KONSTANTIN STEPPED OUT of the car and spoke over the hood. "I do not have a gun," he said. "Please step into the automobile. You will not be harmed."

"What do you think?" Joe asked Frank. Frank shrugged and stared suspiciously at Konstantin.

"You may leave at any time," Konstantin continued. "It is important that we talk. Alone, far from Vladimir and his agents. Your lives may depend upon it."

"Come over here," Frank ordered. Konstantin walked around to the curbside. "Hands on the side of the car. Spread your feet wide apart."

As Konstantin stood in that position, Joe frisked him. "He's clean," Joe said. "No gun, just as he said."

"All right. Get in back." Frank motioned at the back door. "Elena will drive. Joe, you get in the front seat."

"Agreed," Konstantin said as he slid to the far side of the car. Frank got in after him.

The car pulled into traffic.

"Okay," Frank said. "Talk. What do you want?"

"To work with you," Konstantin answered. "To help you, so that you may help me."

The Hardys exchanged surprised glances. "Why would we want to help you?" Joe asked.

"To catch the killer of Martin Chase. Let me come to the point. You and I, we are on the same side, though you do not know it. I am a special operative, dealing with special problems."

His voice deepened. "Problems such as Vladimir."

"What's that to us?" Frank said.

"We have had our eye on Vladimir for some time," Konstantin continued. "Some months ago our agent in London disappeared after suggesting an investigation of Vladimir. His official report never arrived. That made us suspicious."

"I found the report," Frank said. "It was in Vladimir's files. Your agent recommended that Vladimir be recalled."

"You have this file?" Konstantin asked anxiously.

Frank shook his head. "Up in smoke in a bombed car. Go on."

"When Vladimir informed us that an exchange was about to take place, it was decided that I should come here. I arrived during your interrogation and took steps to take over. On determining that you were telling the truth—"

"I don't quite remember it happening that way," Joe said. "Seems to me you were about to fry me."

"He wasn't, Joe," Frank said. "He spoke to the gunmen in English so that we'd understand what he was saying. And he dawdled with the interrogation until we decided to make a break for it. He *wanted* us to escape."

Joe stared. "He *what?*"

Konstantin gazed at Frank with new respect. "Why should I wish that?"

"You want me to guess? I'd say you figured we had the incentive to find the information everyone was looking for, and you wanted us to lead you to it. Am I close?"

"It seems I am a better judge of character than I suspected," Konstantin said, laughing. "Vladimir sees you only as enemies or victims. He failed to see that you have the makings of a fine agent."

"Thanks," Frank said. "Now let's cut to the chase. You still haven't convinced us that we should work with you."

"Ah." Konstantin scratched his head. "I see.

Would it surprise you to know that I already know who the mole is? That I know it is Vladimir.''

"Yeah," Joe said. "We figured that out a long time ago. But convince us to work with you."

"Vladimir is desperate to save himself. That is why he was willing to confront the police."

"I thought that was a little dumb back there at the warehouse. But you seemed as involved as he was," Frank said.

"An act," Konstantin assured them. "If I did not act, he would have grown suspicious. Your escape from me was most convincing. But do you think a trained KGB agent would use such an elementary ploy?"

"Sure," said Frank moodily. He could still feel the grip on his throat, and he hoped the Russian's shins still smarted as well. "I like to think so."

"You would be wrong," Konstantin answered. "Vladimir will not stop until he is safe from you. I think you will also not stop until you find Chase's information, and when you do, I want it. I promise your names will be cleared, and I will prove Vladimir disguised himself as your chauffeur to assassinate Chase and watch you."

"And you get to put Vladimir out of commission," Frank said. "If we agree to work with you, you'll keep the KGB off our backs?"

"Agreed." Konstantin pulled a business card from his pocket. "You can contact me day or night at this number. Have we a deal?"

"We'll let you know," Frank said. "Elena, pull over." The car stopped at a curb and the four of them got out. "You keep up your end as a gesture of good faith, and we'll be in touch."

As he opened the driver's door, Konstantin asked, "Can I trust you?"

"You're such a student of human nature," Frank answered. "You tell me."

Konstantin smiled slowly and shook his head. "You Americans." He climbed into the driver's seat, then leaned over to the passenger's window. "One warning. Do not remain on the streets. The Spanish police are not interested in our deals."

The car pulled away. For long seconds they watched until it disappeared in traffic.

"He's got a point," Joe admitted. "We'd better not hang around where we can be spotted." To Elena he said, "Does the offer to stay with your friends still hold?"

"Of course," Elena said, fear in her voice. "But you said you cannot find the information. How can you make a deal?"

"Konstantin doesn't need to know that," Frank said.

He turned to Joe and Elena. "It's time we changed tactics. If we can't use Martin's information to prove our innocence, we'll use Martin's killer."

"Now that we're pretty sure who he is," Joe said. He stepped into the street to flag down a cab. "I can't wait to see the look on Vladimir's face."

"Neither can I, brother," Frank replied. "I can't wait to see the look on a lot of faces."

The taxi drove down a tree-shaded street, heading toward the house of Elena's friends.

They all sat in the backseat, Elena wedged between the Hardys. Joe stared out the window at the setting sun. Frank, his Walkman over his ears, listened with his eyes closed.

"How can he enjoy himself at a time like this?" Elena asked Joe.

"Music relaxes Frank," Joe explained with a grin. "It helps him think sometimes, and we have to think up a trap for Vladimir in a hurry. We've been lucky so far, but that can't last forever." He turned to look into Elena's eyes. "You've really been a lot of help to us."

She lowered her eyes. "I—they said no one would be hurt. When they tried to hurt you, I had to . . ." Giving in to exhaustion, Elena dropped her head on Joe's shoulder and began to cry. "How could I have trusted them?"

"Because you thought they believed in what you believe in," Joe said softly, putting a comforting arm around her.

The cab pulled up in front of a small house which sat on top of a hill. A long flight of stone steps led up to the house.

Joe let Elena out. "I'll get the fare," he said as she ran up the stairs. Joe reached back into the car and shook Frank. "Come on. We're here."

Frank opened his eyes and took off the headphones as Joe dug into his pocket for money.

Elena rang the doorbell. "Rafael," she called through the door. "It's me. Elena."

The door swung open, and Elena gasped.

"Stand still," said Inspector Melendez, who was standing inside the house. "Did you think the police were unaware of your activities? We have long kept track of your friends." He stepped back into the shadows and stared down at the Hardys. "Signal them to come up. Do not alarm them."

Slowly, forcing a smile, Elena turned. From the street Joe waved, and she waved back.

"Do nothing foolish," Inspector Melendez whispered. "Or you will be jailed in their place."

The inspector's words stinging her ears, Elena continued waving as Frank and Joe started up the stairs.

Chapter

15

ELENA TOOK A deep breath and lowered her hand.

"What are you doing?" Inspector Melendez whispered angrily.

"I will not betray my friends," she said. She cupped her hands around her mouth and shouted down the stairs, "Run! The police are here! Run!" Furious, Inspector Melendez clapped his hand on her shoulder and pulled her into the house.

"Arrest them!" he called out the door. At his command half a dozen policemen leapt from their hiding places among the trees and bushes along the stone steps.

"Melendez," Frank muttered. He glanced at

the cab rolling down the street. It hadn't yet reached the corner. "Let's get out of here."

On the steps Joe hesitated. "Elena—" he began. He could see Inspector Melendez holding her in the doorway as she struggled to break free, but the policemen barred Joe's path.

Frank tugged him back to the sidewalk. "They're cops," Frank said. "Good guys. She'll be all right with them. Come on." The police barreled down at the Hardys.

Joe took a last look at Elena. "We'll be back," he yelled. Then he spun and ran after Frank down the street.

"Taxi!" Frank shouted as he ran. "Wait!"

The taxi came to a stop, then began to back up. Frank and Joe ran to it, opened the doors, and jumped in. *"Vamos! Pronto!"*

Frank flung a fifty-dollar traveler's check on the front seat. "Tell him it's all his if he puts lots of distance between us and Melendez. Hurry."

The cab driver looked at them over his shoulder. His eyes widened as he saw the policemen bearing down on his cab; he slammed his foot down on the gas pedal. With a screech the cab roared away, leaving the policemen coughing and covering their eyes in the cloud of dust kicked up by the tires.

"We've lost them," Frank said, looking out the back window. "They must've parked their cars far away so we wouldn't know they were at the house. By the time they get to them, we'll be long gone.''

"Dóndé?" the driver asked in Spanish as he handed the traveler's check back to Frank. Frank began to sign it.

"Don't worry about the money yet," Joe told his brother. "He wants to know where we're going. I'd like to know that myself."

"Just tell him to drive around for a while." Gloomily, Joe relayed the message. "As long as the cops didn't get the license number, we're as safe here as anywhere. What's eating you?"

"I wish we didn't have to leave Elena like that," Joe replied. "She shouldn't have been caught."

"I'm sure Melendez will let her go once we prove we're innocent," Frank said. "If there's no crime, there're no grounds for holding her."

"That's kind of optimistic, isn't it?" said Joe. "Frank, we've never been in as bad a spot as this. Even if we live there's no way we can stay out of jail. We've run out all our leads."

"We can't give up," Frank said. "I know we're overlooking something. Let me think." He put on his headphones and slipped a Rolling Stones cassette into his tape player.

"Listening to music isn't going to help," Joe continued, although he knew Frank could barely hear him. "What are we overlooking? We can't go searching all over anyway. Every cop in Málaga is after us, and probably every Russian in the south of Spain—except Konstantin. And him I wouldn't trust any farther than I could throw him.''

Frank leaned his head back and closed his eyes, the steady throb of rock music beating in his head. The cab cruised aimlessly, heading west out of the city.

"And don't forget we've probably gotten the Gray Man in trouble, and the Network wants to hang us out to dry,'' Joe said as Frank hummed softly. "We're stuck in a foreign country with no way out. I don't see how we're going to walk away from this one.''

Frank began to laugh.

"I don't see that there's anything to laugh about,'' Joe said.

Frank pulled off the headphones and grinned at his brother. "I do. I just figured out where the information is.''

"What? Where? Let's go get it.''

"That's the best part,'' Frank said. "There's no need to.'' He glanced out the window as they passed a road sign. "What did that say? Torremolinos?''

Joe nodded. "Four miles away, yeah. Are you going to tell me, or what?''

"Trust me,'' Frank replied. "Torremolinos is where Vladimir's house is. Tell the driver to head there.''

His smile got grimmer. "We're going mole hunting."

Like the rest of the towns on the Costa del Sol, Torremolinos was a resort town. Though far smaller than Málaga, the town had many discos that glittered under the Mediterranean night sky.

By late evening the Hardys stood in front of the Tortuga Club. Built of stone and stucco, water stains smeared its outer walls, and Joe wrinkled his nose in disgust.

"The cab driver told us this was the worst disco in the town," he said. "Why did you insist that he bring us here?"

"We don't want a place with a lot of people," Frank explained. He pulled open the door and they went in. "But they'd better have a phone in here."

"Over there," Joe said, pointing to a dark alcove off the door. He stopped. No music was playing. Only a waitress and a disc jockey were in the whole place.

"Want to tell me what's going on?" Joe asked.

"Take a table," Frank said, and Joe sat at a table just to the left of the door. Frank took out Konstantin's card. "I've got to make a couple of calls," he said, walking to the phone.

Several minutes passed as Frank made call after call, and Joe watched curiously. A couple entered, ordered drinks, finished them, and left.

The waitress hovered around Joe, waiting for an order, but Joe smiled uncertainly until she went away. At long last Frank returned.

"What was all that about?" Joe asked. "Who were you calling?"

"I started with Konstantin," Frank began.

"Konstantin?" Joe stared at his brother. "Are you out of your mind? We should be trying to get in touch with the Gray Man."

"We don't know how," Frank reminded him. "With his connections, I'm sure he'll arrive about the time Melendez and Vladimir get here."

"I think maybe I'm missing something," Joe said. "You'd better explain."

"I called both Melendez and Vladimir and told them we'd be here at midnight to turn over the information that will clear us," Frank said, looking at his watch. It read 10:25. "I told Vladimir to come alone. Melendez is bringing Elena."

"Great!" Joe said, his eyes brightening. Then a look of doubt swept over his face. "So they all come here at once. How will that help us?"

"Konstantin's coming right over. He's going to bait the trap for us." Frank eyed the disc jockey. "We should get some music going. You think the deejay takes requests?" He got up and walked to the far end of the floor just as Konstantin stormed in.

There was a flush of excitement on Konstantin's face, but when he saw Joe, he calmed down and walked over to his table.

"You have good news?" he asked.

"Your guess is as good as mine," Joe replied. He waved a thumb at Frank, who was deep in conversation with the disc jockey. "Ask him."

As the sound of the Rolling Stones filled the room, Frank came back and sat down. "We found what Martin left us," he said.

"We did?" said Joe.

From his pocket Frank dug two Rolling Stones cassette cases. He slid them across the table to Konstantin. "Identical in every way. Except I had one copy when I left New York and two after Martin used my tape player." He opened one of the cases. It was empty. He put it into his pocket. "The deejay's playing my tape. The other tape has Martin's info. I didn't know it until I took the tapes from the police warehouse."

Konstantin slowly tapped his forehead, thinking, then dropped a finger on top of the remaining case. "Ingenious. You have listened to the tape?"

Frank shook his head. "I thought I'd leave that to you."

"Good." With a flick of his wrist Konstantin flung the case open. The cassette inside crashed to the floor. Before Joe or Frank could react, he stamped it with his heel, tearing tape and sending bits of plastic flying in all directions.

"Much better. So much off my mind," the Russian said.

Joe stared from Konstantin to the wrecked cassette on the floor, his eyes growing wide with sudden realization. "It was you," he said slowly. "Vladimir isn't the mole! It was you all along."

Chapter

16

JOE LUNGED ACROSS the table, grabbing at Konstantin. The Russian's laughter faded, and from under the table came the telltale click of a revolver hammer being cocked. Joe froze, his fingers inches from Konstantin. And trembling with frustration, he let his hands fall back to the table.

"Sit down," Konstantin said. Joe sat. A dozen men and women came in together, smiling and laughing, and walked past the table to the dance floor. "Do not move. Do not attempt to speak to anyone," the Russian warned.

"What are you going to do with us?" Joe asked.

"We'll disappear," Frank said. "Just like our

chauffeur disappeared. You'd know more about that than we would, right, Konstantin?''

Konstantin gave him a cold stare.

''Funny how you knew about him,'' Frank continued. ''We told the Gray Man about our chauffeur, and we told the Spanish police. But we never told Vladimir. And we never told you. There's only one way you could know.''

''You're right,'' said Joe, studying Konstantin as if seeing him for the first time. ''Dark wig, fake mustache, sunglasses. *Konstantin* was our chauffeur!''

''Shut up,'' Konstantin said.

''What are you going to do? Kill us here?'' Frank asked as another group entered. ''You'll have a lot of witnesses. It won't do much good to save yourself from the KGB only to have the Spanish police throw you in jail for the rest of your life. Seems to me we have a stalemate.''

A man from one of the groups stepped to the bar and ordered a drink. Like his friends, he was dressed in tight black slacks and a bright silky shirt. But his hair had gone prematurely gray.

As he picked up his drink, he turned slightly and raised it to Frank and Joe, catching their eyes. Before Konstantin noticed, he turned back to the bar.

It was the Gray Man.

''No stalemate,'' Konstantin replied. ''I would prefer not to cause trouble here. But should it be

127

necessary, I can be out of the country within the hour. Please do not force my hand.''

"It won't work," Joe said. "Frank called Melendez and Vladimir, and they'll be here any minute. You don't have time to do anything to us. You barely have time to get away.''

Konstantin cocked an eyebrow. "You arranged for both to arrive at the same time?''

"That's right," Frank said confidently.

"Did you not think I would have Vladimir's phone monitored?" Konstantin said, looking at his watch. "You told Vladimir you would meet him at midnight. It is now ten to eleven. No, they will not arrive in time to save you.''

His revolver glinted for an instant in the light from the revolving mirrored ball. He deftly transferred the gun to his jacket pocket, keeping his finger on the trigger. "Up," he said. "Time to go.''

Frank looked over his shoulder at the door. "And if we don't?" he asked calmly. The outline of the gun appeared in Konstantin's pocket.

"Then you die now," Konstantin replied.

Joe sprang from his seat, his hands gripping the edge of the table, and as he stood, he began to tip the table into Konstantin. It didn't budge. He looked down to see Konstantin's foot pressed down on one of the table's feet, keeping it from moving.

"I am ready for any trick," Konstantin said.

He motioned again for Frank to rise, but Frank stayed in his chair.

"I should probably tell you the Gray Man is standing to your right," Frank said.

"A desperate lie," Konstantin said, his eyes fixed on Frank. "Get up."

"You found me out," Frank answered, pretending to be exasperated. "I lied about the Gray Man. I lie about everything. I even lied about not listening to the tape."

Konstantin looked puzzled. "You knew? Then why—"

The Gray Man started to rush Konstantin, but before he could reach him, the Russian spun, pulling his gun from his pocket. He aimed it at the form running toward him.

Joe slapped out, driving Konstantin's hand down, and with a crack a bullet smacked into the disco floor. The Gray Man slammed against Konstantin, knocking him off his feet and throwing him back against the wall.

At the sound of the gunshot, the music stopped. The couples on the dance floor stared at the three men grappling at the table. Then slowly their attention was directed toward the door.

Vladimir and eight Russians rushed in, guns drawn. When he saw Konstantin fighting with the Gray Man, Vladimir snarled rapid orders to his agents. They moved toward the table.

Frank stood.

All at once a voice came over the loudspeakers. "A top agent for the KGB has actually been a mole working for the Chinese for the last eight years," Martin's voice said. "His name is Konstantin. He was recruited while still in training by Wong Wah Lum, head of China's Third Directorate. Konstantin has since—"

Joe, Vladimir, the Gray Man, Konstantin, and the Russian agents stopped and listened as the voice droned on, outlining Konstantin's acts of treason against the Soviet Union.

Then the voice broke off, replaced by the sound of Konstantin speaking to someone in Chinese and a Chinese voice answering him. By the look on their faces, Frank knew both the Gray Man and Vladimir had recognized the voice of the man called Wong Wah Lum.

Konstantin looked icily at Frank. "You—all the time you—" Fiercely, he kicked aside the wrecked cassette on the floor. "You gave me the wrong tape."

Frank nodded. "Yeah, I sort of lied about that too."

Vladimir pointed to Konstantin. "Take him." He looked over at Frank, Joe, and the Gray Man. "Them too."

"Halt!" came a commanding voice from the doorway. It was Inspector Melendez accompanied by a small army of policemen. He held out his badge for everyone to see. "You are all under arrest."

"Policía!" someone on the dance floor cried out, and in panic the dancers rushed for the door, scattering the policemen. Vladimir clapped his hands, and his agents spread out across the bar. Policemen raced in to grab them.

"I can clear everything up," the Gray Man called to Inspector Melendez. But as he turned his head, Konstantin decked him. The Russian moved for the door. Vladimir flung himself into Konstantin, grabbing the tall Russian around the waist. And Konstantin rammed his fists against Vladimir's back.

In the midst of all this, Inspector Melendez spied the Hardys. "You have made a good run of it, but you are finally caught." He reached for them, but Joe overturned the table, hurling it into the police officer's path.

"That's the guy you want, Inspector," Frank said, pointing at Konstantin. *"He* killed Martin. We have to go."

Vladimir and Konstantin came stumbling by like a pair of clumsy dancers doing a waltz. Frank leaned forward, pushing them both toward Inspector Melendez. Then he grabbed a chair and threw it through a window. Before the inspector could push through to them, Frank and Joe had climbed through the broken window and landed on the street outside.

"What are we running for?" Joe asked. "They've got Konstantin. It's all over."

"Not quite," Frank said. He looked down the street, empty when they entered the disco but now lined with police cars and autos with diplomatic plates. A policeman stood vigilantly outside one of the police cars. Inside, in the back seat, sat Elena. Frank tossed Joe a ring of keys.

"What are these?" Joe asked, amazed.

"Vladimir's keys. I took them from him when he passed by," Frank said. "Get Elena and Vladimir's car. I'll distract the cop."

Joe crept along the line of cars, staying out of the policeman's sight. From the disco the sounds of fighting continued. The noise caught the policeman's attention, and nervously he drummed his fingers on the squad car's dashboard.

From his hiding place down the street, Frank called to the policeman. The policeman looked around but saw nothing. Frank called again, louder. The policeman got out of the car.

Joe popped his head in the window on the opposite side of the car, startling Elena. He put a finger to his lips, warning her to be silent. Frank called again, and Joe opened the car door with a soft click. Elena slid over and crept from the car. Signing for her to crouch, Joe led her away. They ducked out of sight behind a limousine as the policeman returned to his car.

"Which car is Vladimir's?" Joe whispered. A

shrill police whistle pierced the air. Elena pointed out a BMW on the other side of the street, and they all ran to it. In seconds Joe unlocked the doors and they slid in, Elena taking the wheel. She put a key in the ignition and turned it.

The ignition wouldn't budge.

She tried another key, frantically watching in the mirror as the policeman began a car-by-car search for her. "It will not work," she said, trying another and another. Finally, she tossed the ring in Joe's lap, reached under the dashboard, and brought out two wires. She touched them together. The car started.

"Where'd you learn to do that?" Joe asked, as the car pulled onto the street. Ahead, Frank stood in the road, waving at them.

"American television," she replied. The policeman spotted the car and began to run beside it, grabbing at the handles.

"If we stop, he'll catch us," Joe said. They raced toward Frank. Joe reached over the back seat, unlatched the back door, and flung it open. "You'll have to jump for it," he yelled at Frank through his open window.

As the car passed, Frank leapt, snatching at the doorframe. His heels scraped the pavement as he was dragged along, and, straining, he drew his knees up to his chest, lifting his feet off the ground. Twisting, he swung into the back seat of the BMW and slammed the door behind him.

"Glad you could make it," Joe quipped. "Mind telling me *now* what's going on?"

"In a minute, Joe," Frank said. "Elena, you mentioned Vladimir had a house in Torremolinos. Know where it is?"

"Yes," Elena said.

"Great. Take us there," he replied. "Sorry I couldn't let you in on my plan, Joe. I wanted you to react the way you did in front of Konstantin."

"Let me guess," Joe said. "When you realized what the tape was, you gave it to the disc jockey with instructions to play it over the loudspeakers when you gave the signal."

"Right," Frank said. "He had his own Stones album to play, so it seemed like I gave him the real Stones tape. When I stood up, Martin's tape went on. All I had to do was stall until Vladimir and Melendez got there."

"Good thing they were early."

Frank grinned. "No, they were right when I expected them. If you were trying to catch someone, and they said they'd meet you in a certain place at a certain time, wouldn't you try to get there first? I figured if I told them midnight, they'd be there by eleven."

"I still don't understand what we're doing," Joe said. "Everyone heard the tape. They know Konstantin's the mole, and when it all gets put together, Melendez will let us off the murder charge. So why did we need Elena, and why did we take Vladimir's car?"

"Because it's not over," Frank answered. "The Network played us for fools. Wouldn't you like to pay them back?"

Joe smacked a fist into his other hand. "I sure would."

"This business started because the Network was trying to trade for one of their agents. Now that the tape's public knowledge, it's useless as trade. But Vladimir still has the Network's agent."

"I get it," Joe said. "Vladimir would have him stashed somewhere near, but not in the consulate. So the likeliest place would be—"

"His house," Elena interrupted. They neared a two-story house with curved red tiles on the roof. Around the house was a gate, and as the car approached, a man stepped out of the gate and shut it behind him. He held out his palm, signaling the car to stop.

"Right," Frank said. "We needed Elena to show us where the house was, and Vladimir's car to get us through the front gate. Stay cool."

The car rolled to a stop, and the man, carrying a machine gun, walked up to Elena's window. "Vladimir told us to wait inside," Elena said, bluffing.

The man studied them for several moments,

then said something in Russian, his finger nervously tightening on the trigger.

"What does he say?" Elena asked, puzzled.

"He's on to us," Frank began. "Hit it—"

His words were cut off as a hail of bullets ripped into the car.

Chapter

17

THE BULLETS DENTED metal and smacked against glass, but they all bounced off.

"Vladimir must have bulletproofed his car too!" Frank said. "Quick! Roll up your window!" he ordered Elena.

But she sat, trembling, as if she'd never heard Frank speak. The man outside started turning his gun on the open spot. Joe reached over Elena, slapping the window control. The bulletproof glass rose swiftly.

"Hold on," Joe cried. From the passenger seat he stepped hard on the gas pedal and grabbed the steering wheel. The BMW lurched forward, speeding toward the gate.

Frank flung his door open. It clipped the man outside as they passed, knocking him off his feet.

He didn't get up. The car crashed through the gate and careened toward the house.

"The brake," Frank shouted. "Hit the brake!"

"I can't," Joe said. "It's too far. Elena!"

All at once Elena snapped her head up. She's in shock, Joe realized. "Elena! Get with it! Hit the brake!" Gasping in surprise, she seized the wheel and slammed on the brake.

The BMW skidded sideways and smashed into a glass-enclosed porch. In a flurry of shattered glass and scattered furniture, it came to a stop.

"Everyone okay?" Frank asked.

"I am," Joe replied. Elena still held the steering wheel, staring straight ahead and shaking. "I think Elena's had better times, but she wasn't hurt." He patted her on the shoulder, and she turned fearful eyes toward him. "Stay here and calm down, Elena. Honk the horn if you see anyone coming."

"She'll be all right," Frank said as he and Joe got out of the car. "We all are, thanks to Vladimir's mania for security."

In the light by the gate Joe could see the armed man's chest rising and falling rhythmically. "He's okay too. Just knocked out."

"Good," Frank said. "Let's go. If there's anyone inside, they couldn't have missed all that noise." He darted into the house. It was simpler than Frank had expected. Just a porch, small dining room, tiled foyer, and sunken living room. There was a tiled stair leading to the second floor.

At the top of the stairs were two Russians. One was slender, but the other bulged with muscles and stood over six feet tall. At a command from the slender man, the big man started down the stairs.

"Trouble?" Joe asked as he caught up with Frank. He spied the giant lurching toward them. Trouble, he thought.

The slender man disappeared down the hall.

"There's no time to waste," Frank said. Together, the Hardys sprinted up the stairs, startling the huge Russian.

He grabbed for Frank, and Joe slammed into him, making him stagger back. Frank ducked under the giant's grasp, stepped past him on the stairs, and slammed his fists against the back of the Russian's knees. The big man's legs buckled, and he toppled.

His hand reached out and caught Joe's shirt-sleeve. Over and over they tumbled down the stairs, landing with a thud in the foyer. Frank looked at the twisted bodies below. Neither moved.

"Joe!" Frank called. He started back down the stairs. "Joe!"

Joe, dazed by the fall, lifted his head. "Don't worry about me. Go." He flashed his brother a pained grin, and Frank dashed to the upper landing to follow the slender man. Joe began to disentangle himself from the giant.

The giant lashed out, clamping his hand around Joe's throat. Joe clawed uselessly at the Russian's wrist, and as the Russian stood, he lifted Joe off his feet.

Joe let go of the giant's wrist and clapped his palms as hard as he could against the Russian's ears. The Russian dropped Joe to the floor and cupped his hands against his head. Joe scrambled to his feet.

But with a sweep of his hand the Russian knocked Joe back into the living room against the fireplace. The giant charged at him.

Joe bounded to his feet, backing away from the Russian's punches. "There's no need to fight," Joe said. "My brother has everything under control upstairs, so you've already lost. Let's just call it quits, okay?"

Smirking, the giant raised a meaty fist and swung down at Joe. Joe dived and tackled the Russian. With an astonished look the huge man fell forward and cracked his head into an armor breastplate hanging on the wall. He twirled twice, then crashed to the floor.

Relieved and exhausted, Joe slumped against a wall and wondered what had become of his brother.

*   *   *

Frank Hardy kicked open a door. It was one of four on the top floor, but behind it was neither the slender Russian nor the Network's agent. He unclenched his fists. The room was virtually a duplicate of Vladimir's office in the consulate, down to the file cabinets and the heavy oak desk. He checked the center door on the desk, and it slid open. He smiled. Inside were several small black books. Remember what you're here for, he told himself, though he suspected the room held a lot of information.

Almost absentmindedly, he pocketed the black books and left the room. Something moved at the opposite end of the hall, and he ducked back into the office. Frank did not understand the Russian words he heard, but the tone was clear. Hands raised, he stepped back into the hall.

At the far end stood the slender Russian, holding a pistol to the head of another man. The prisoner was slightly taller than the slender KGB agent, and his face was covered with an unruly thatch of beard. His hands were tied behind his back, and strips of surgical tape covered his eyes and mouth. Judging from the paleness of the man's skin, Frank guessed he'd been kept out of the sun a long time.

"The Network's man, I presume?" Frank said. In answer, the Russian aimed his gun at Frank's chest, and his finger tightened on the trigger.

Suddenly the Network agent's head lashed

back, and his skull conked the Russian's jaw. Frank sprang down the hall. The prisoner stepped aside, and Frank spun, kicking out with his foot. The slender Russian collapsed.

"You're the American agent?" Frank asked as he helped the second man to his feet. He ripped the tape from the man's face. "What's your name?"

The man nodded. "My code name's Donner. It's about time the Network sent someone for me." His eyes slit with suspicion. "You should know that. Aren't you from the Network?"

"Yes and no," Frank replied. He unknotted the cords binding Donner's wrists, and Donner rubbed the circulation back into his hands. "It's a long story. We'll fill you in on the way out."

Donner limped slightly as they headed downstairs, and Frank offered him an arm. At the foot of the stairs they found Joe, patiently waiting.

"What took you so long?" Joe said.

"That's just what *he* said," Frank replied, waving a thumb at Donner. "Everyone's a wise guy."

"Who are you?" Donner asked as they cut through the dining room.

"I'm Joe Hardy, and this is my brother, Frank," Joe said. They moved across the ruined patio, heading for the wrecked BMW.

"I've heard of you," Donner said. "The Gray Man's protégés. You're supposed to be untrustworthy."

142

"If you don't trust us, you can always stay here," Frank suggested, but Donner winced and shook his head. Elena came out of the car as they approached. "Let's get to safety before anyone else shows up."

They ran to the gate. The man they had left there still lay on the ground, unconscious. They passed through the gate and onto the darkened street.

"We did it," Joe said. "We showed the Network how it's done."

"Wait!" Donner shouted, but it was too late. The night exploded in light, blinding them, and as Frank's eyes refocused, he saw they were caught in a semicircle of car headlights. There was nowhere for them to go but back. A bald man stepped from one of the cars.

"Very good," Vladimir said with cold pleasure. "Now I have you all."

Chapter

18

"YOU ARE MY prisoners," Vladimir declared, a satisfied smile on his face.

"What do you need us for?" Joe asked. He stepped between Donner and Vladimir. "You've got the name you wanted; we've got the Network's man. That was the deal."

"Silence," Vladimir said. "The exchange never took place. I am not bound by that bargain." He snapped his fingers, and two Russians shoved Konstantin into the semicircle of light. The blond man curled his lip in rage, but Vladimir laughed.

"You have given me much more than a name," Vladimir continued, staring Joe in the eye. "For the capture of this one"—like a circus barker, he swept his arm extravagantly, motioning at Konstantin—"I will become a hero of the state, with pay to match." His eyes flashed with anger. "But you annoy me, young man. You disrupt my plans, destroy my car, invade my house. You are too dangerous, you and your brother. I must be rid of you."

Vladimir pointed at Donner and Elena. "Take them." Two Russians stepped into the circle of light and grabbed them, forcing them to Konstantin's side. "They have further uses." He grinned at the Hardys. "But *these* two—"

"I'm surprised you managed to get out of the disco in one piece," Frank said. "You must be better than I thought to get away from Melendez."

"Yes." Vladimir glared at him icily. "Escape was a simple matter." He patted his coat pocket. "And I now have the tape. I have Konstantin. I have all I need.

"I do not need *you*." Two Russians appeared on either side of Vladimir. "Take them somewhere and dispose of them."

Two shots rang out, and the headlights of the car Vladimir stood next to spat glass and went dark. Desperate to stay out of the line of fire, Vladimir threw himself to the ground.

"No one goes anywhere," the Gray Man said from the darkness. His voice seemed to come from all directions at once. Frank and Joe could see no sign of him. "Didn't you think I'd follow you, Vlad? Let Donner, the Hardys, and the girl go."

"You are forgetting," Vladimir said. "My men have the Hardys in their sights. Show yourself or they will kill the boys."

"I have *you* in my sights," the still-invisible Gray Man said. "This is a Sterling assault rifle. I could put three bullets in you before you finish telling your men to shoot them. Is that the way you want to play it?"

Vladimir licked his lips thoughtfully. He waved his men back. "And if I give you these four," he called to the Gray Man, "I keep Konstantin?"

"Sounds fair."

"Wait!" Konstantin suddenly called out. He shook himself free of his captors. "Gray Man! I wish to defect!"

Vladimir sputtered, unable to find words to voice his anger. From the darkness the Gray Man said, "You killed Martin, right?"

"Of course," Konstantin casually admitted. "You would have done the same in my place. I wish to defect."

"You make a big mistake, Konstantin. You and I aren't alike at all," the Gray Man retorted. "I don't like moles, and I don't like killers. If I had my way, I'd send you back to your KGB masters and let them deal with you." There was a long pause. "But you can tell us a lot about both Chinese and Russian espionage, and I can't overlook that. All right, I'll help you defect, but you try anything and you'll be sorry."

"No!" Vladimir shouted, and he lunged forward, grabbing Frank. "Konstantin stays here! If I were to lose him, I would suffer in his place." A spring-operated knife popped out of his sleeve and into his hand. He pressed it against Frank's throat as they backed toward the wall. "Shoot now if you choose, Gray Man. You will hit your friend, not me. And my men will gun down your other friends. Give up."

"Seems to me like you have a stalemate," Frank said, feeling the cool sharp touch of steel on his throat. He reached into his pocket and came out with a small black book. "Maybe this can break it."

Vladimir stared, then inhaled sharply as he recognized what Frank held. "My bankbooks." Enraged, he prodded Frank under the chin with the point of the knife. "Where did you get this?"

"Same place as all the others," Frank replied. "There were a lot of them, and they all seemed to refer to bank accounts. Lots of bank accounts. Skimming funds from the KGB, Vladimir?"

Vladimir said nothing.

"Yeah, that's what I thought," Frank said. "That's why the KGB's London man reported you, isn't it? Your own private retirement fund, at KGB expense."

Vladimir's arm fell away from Frank.

"Let us go, and I'll tell you where the other bankbooks are."

The knife slid from Vladimir's fingers and clattered on the ground. "Let them go," Vladimir ordered wearily. He was a beaten man, Frank knew. "Let them all go."

"Uh-oh," Joe said. "Frank, I think you overplayed our hand." Beyond the semicircle of light the other Russian agents moved forward. Two roughly shoved Elena and Donner at Vladimir and the Hardys, and a second later Konstantin joined them.

"You are traitors," a Russian outside the circle said to Konstantin and Vladimir as the others took aim. To everyone in the light he said, "You are all enemies of the state. Ready—aim—"

An arc of light ripped through the night, exposing and blinding the Gray Man and the Russians. "This is the police," came a deep Spanish-accented voice over a bullhorn. "Drop your weapons and put your hands up."

Two Russians spun and trained their weapons on the voice. Two shots exploded from the night, and the Russians jerked back, flopping to the ground. When the other Russians and the Gray Man had let their guns fall, a tall, burly man with dark hair walked into the light.

"Inspector Melendez," Joe cried. "I never thought I'd say this, but am I glad to see *you*."

"You are all," the inspector replied, "under arrest."

Frank left the ticket counter and pushed his way through the airport crowds. Ahead, Joe chatted with the Gray Man, and as he caught his brother's attention, Frank waved the tickets at him. As Frank reached them, the Gray Man was saying, "It's all cleared up. Good thing Melendez was already listening when Konstantin admitted to killing Martin. That made it much easier to get you off the hook."

"I thought you had it planned like that," Joe said.

"Don't I wish! Sometimes you just get lucky."

"Yeah, it's about time," Joe answered. "You just make sure the Network knows we beat them at their own game. They couldn't shake Donner free and we *did*. Let them think about that the next time they want to take us for a ride."

"I don't think that'll happen again," the Gray Man said. "Donner told me to say goodbye, by the way. He's got his hands full right now."

"Is he taking care of Konstantin's defection?" Frank asked.

"No," the Gray Man replied. "Konstantin's staying here to stand trial for Martin's murder. That was part of our deal with Melendez. No, the person defecting is Vladimir."

"*What?*" said both Hardys in unison.

The Gray Man chuckled. "He feels he'd be safer in the decadent West, especially with his bank balance." He spotted two familiar figures entering the airport. "Company coming."

"Elena!" Joe shouted as she ran to him. Behind her Inspector Melendez walked at a steady pace.

Frank cocked his head at Joe and Elena. "Let's let them say goodbye to each other." He picked up the suitcases and, sandwiched between the two men, started for the departure gate.

"I'm surprised you came by to see us off," Frank told Inspector Melendez.

"I wished to be certain you were truly leaving," Inspector Melendez answered, a trace of a smile on his lips. "If you should ever choose to return to Spain—"

"Yes?"

"Do me a favor. Go to Italy," the inspector concluded. "Goodbye, Frank Hardy. Say goodbye to your brother for me." Frank and Inspector Melendez shook hands, and without another word Inspector Melendez turned and left.

Joe ran up as the line of passengers began filtering onto the plane. After a quick round of farewells with the Gray Man, they joined the line and headed up the ramp to the plane. Within minutes they were seated.

Frank took his Walkman from his suitcase and put it on as the plane taxied out to the runway.

"Sorry the vacation got cut short," he said apologetically to Joe.

"It's okay," Joe replied. "We met girls, we went swimming, we went boating, we saw a lot of scenery and sights. I've had enough vacationing for a lifetime."

Frank smiled and slipped on his headphones. Joe put his head back and closed his eyes. As the plane left the ground, Joe dreamed of Bayport and its quaint, quiet streets. He was looking forward to going home, he realized.

He would finally get to relax!

Frank and Joe's next case:

Greg and Mike Rawley are the new boys at Bayport High. Adopted by the wealthy Walter Rawley, the boys fit in just a little too well. Rivalry develops between them and the Hardys when Callie Shaw grows fond of Greg, and Mike is a challenge to Joe on the football field.

Then Greg and Mike's mother, Linda, discovers the diary of Rawley's first wife. The diary leads Linda Rawley to suspect her mild-mannered husband of being a spy, or even a murderer. Did the late Mrs. Rawley really die of natural causes?

Fearing for their mother's welfare, Greg and Mike turn to the Hardys for help. And when Linda Rawley is kidnapped, Frank and Joe pose as her sons. Could this turn into a very lethal family affair? Find out in *Blood Relations*, Case #15 in The Hardy Boys Casefiles.